ZOMBIES

ON

A

PLANE

ZOMBIES ON A PLANE

STILL ALIVE

BOOK THREE

Javan Bonds

Copyright © 2017 Javan Bonds &
If I Only Had A Monkey Publishing

All rights reserved. No portion of this book may be reproduced in any form without permission from the publisher, except as permitted by U.S. copyright law.
For permissions contact: ifionlyhadamonkey@gmail.com

Cover by Covers by Christian
www.coversbychristian.com

ISBN-13: 978-1542803991
ISBN-10: 1542803993

Acknowledgments

Thanks to my parents. I wouldn't have been able to publish these works without my dad. I would have been nagged a lot less about my vulgarisms if my mom was not my alpha reader.

Thanks to my phenomenal editor at Swift Creative Writing, Sheila Shedd. I wouldn't be the writer I am today without her tutelage.

Thanks to my beta readers, Dr. Larry Johnston, Kao Kikuyama, Glen Mardis (Peevie Claus), Mandy Owens, and Taft Reeves.

Thanks to my final proofreader, Donna Shields. It's always good to have an extra set of eyes read over my drivel.

Thanks to my hero, the original inspiration for this series and the author of the foreword for this book, Mark Tufo. If not for Zombie Fallout, you would not be reading Still Alive.

Thanks to Rhiannon Frater, Seanan McGuire (Mira Grant), ZA Recht, and all the others that keep me entertained while I'm writing.

Thanks to Akambiya Mwanza, my real life Zambian friend. She is the physical inspiration for Aka and helped me with some of the Zambian culture. See? I really do know black people!

Thanks to my bodybuilder brother, Ethan Bonds. He is the inspiration for Easy and everything you read about the character is Ethan, besides the lack of a sense of humor.

Thanks to Christian. Not only for the awesome cover design, but for the hilarity his translations from English provide.

Javan Bonds

Disclaimer

THIS IS A work of fiction. Names, characters, places, and incidents either are the product of the author's imagination or are used fictitiously, and any resemblances to persons, living or dead, business establishments, events, or locales are entirely coincidental.

Foreword

What is it about Z-Poc books that keeps them going, keeps readers devouring them the minute they hit the shelves? I mean, with all that work out there you'd think we would have covered all possible scenarios and outcomes and we'd be prepared for the end and the monsters and battles…but that's just it…we don't know what to expect. We need new writers, new stories, fresh blood, and most of all, original monsters to keep us looking forward to that day we all get to fight for survival.

That's what's great about Javan Bonds' *Still Alive* series; it's a strikingly new, extremely twisted perspective on the End of Days–that, and it's damned funny. Even when faced with naked, filthy, cannibals leaving a trail of excrement behind them, Bonds' main character and chronicler, Mo Collins, still has "man problems" to deal with. Fighting these progressively cognizant "Peevies" (plague victims) by night and his own frustrations with parents, his love life, and his own apathy by day, Mo is the perfect Every Guy. You gotta root for him.

Javan's series has some wild scenes of gore, and that's just his sex life…the zombies are even more disgusting. His life and characters are mimicking a movie plot, which is a cool tie-in to our other favorite medium, and he thinks his destiny might be written.

But guess what, Mo? It isn't. Win or die, that's on us whether we travel with a Prophet or go it alone. Collins' journey is just beginning, and it's an exciting, unexpectedly original one.

Plus, you know, how cool is it to live on a replica pirate ship?

Mark Tufo

Horror Author of the Award Winning Zombie Fallout series and Highest rated Author on Goodreads

Cast of Characters

(In Order Of Appearance)

Elmo "Mo" Collins: The Hero and Chronicler. Acting Captain of the *Viva Ancora;* Jack of No Trades.

Crow: Cook and Crewmate on the Viva Ancora. Permanent Resident Fisherwoman. Given name later discovered to be Rose.

Marlon "Smokes" Williamson: The Oracle. Gangbanger, Dope Dealer (Ret.); Interpreter and Channeler of The Screenwriter.

Petunia "Hammer" Sledge: The Expert. Captain, US Marine Corp, Special Ops (Ret). Owner of Bottom Dollar Pawn; Extreme Survivalist.

Gene Stanley: The Tech. PhD Mechanical Engineering (pending); Owner, Excelsior Comics and Collectables; Collector of Fantasy/Science Fiction Memorabilia.

Bradley Gage: The Old Friend. National Champion Sharpshooter, Paraplegic Trainer and Bodybuilder.

Mary: The Innocent. Capuchin Monkey, Service Animal (partnered with Bradley.) Clearly wise compared to most of the other characters.

Cast of Characters Continued

Sarah Ogle: The Love Interest. Longtime Friend and Love-of-His-Life to Mo.

Randy Collins: Leader of The Similar (Former). Mo's Father, Interim Mayor of the Island of Guntersville; Amateur Survivalist.

Debbie (Mrs.) Collins: The Hero's Mother. Conservative Matriarch. Never uses nicknames.

Dr. Philip George: The Medicine Man. Cardiologist, Indian, discovered to be Phantom commander in the Indian NSG. Sniper.

Tychus Jones: The Loner. Janitor and Sharp shooter National Guardsman (Ret.) Owner of house cat, Adjutant.

Ezekiel "Easy" Collins: Mo's brother. Bodybuilder and extreme health enthusiast. The Protector and Nursing degree (pending).

Akambiya "Aka" Ngona: Easy's fiancée. Dam Technician and Nursing degree (pending).

The Phantom HITs: Kumar, Mahatma, Rejesh and Sanjay. Subordinates of Dr. George, Indian NSG commandos.

Cast of Characters Continued

Georgia Daniels: wife of The Builder (deceased). Love Interest to Gene, Mother of Hunter.

Earl Buckalew: The Betrayer, missing and presumed dead after leaving Bottom Dollar just after May Day. Aligns himself with The Villian.

Cheryl Slice: The Dictator. Warden of the Joseph A. Davidson State Correctional Facility,

Captain Jonathan Bobbit: The Villian. U S Army officer, Megalomaniac.

Sojourner "Soje" Williamson: The Man of God. Farmer, Preacher. Patriarch of the Williamson Clan.

Annihilation has no terrors for me, because I have already tried it before I was born–a hundred million years–and I have suffered more in an hour, in this life, than I remember to have suffered in the whole hundred million years put together.

Mark Twain

Zombies On A Plane

Prologue

"THIS IS CLARK Carson, reporting live from the city of Guntersville. It's the city's first annual Cinco de Mayo parade and celebration. US 431 has been diverted to northbound traffic only to help in the evacuation from an outbreak of a highly contagious flu bug originating from Mobile, so the festivities that were scheduled for Gunter Avenue have been moved to Sunset Drive. We are standing right across from Civitan Park."

The cameraman panned to the right, showing large groups of spectators lining the road. There were people sitting along the sidewalk in lawn chairs, a large tent selling Mexican flags, and vendors selling ice cream and various other treats and merchandise. Though a bit cloudy, it was warm and not too humid; most would call it a perfect day.

Ranchero music began playing as the first float-carrying truck rounded the bend. The camera zoomed in on a paper-mâché sombrero with children throwing candy from the sides.

Before the next truck could be seen, viewers could hear a woman screaming in terrible pain from somewhere off-camera.

The cameras spun to the parking lot in front of Piggly Wiggly. A woman was being attacked by what appeared to be a pale blue, naked man. He was on top of her, leaning in to kiss, or bite, the woman on the neck. She let out another scream, and before she had even closed her mouth, her attacker was already up, running to tackle another shopper.

The woman used her buggy to keep the man at bay while she drew a pistol from her purse. This being Alabama, it wasn't surprising that she was carrying. The lunatic just shoved the buggy out of the way and was about to pounce when she put five bullets into his chest.

The reporter mumbled something off screen and the camera cut back to him. "This is Clark Carson, reporting live from Guntersville. We just witnessed an obviously deranged man assault a woman at the Piggly Wiggly.

Zombies On A Plane

He ran from his first victim to attack another shopper, unprovoked, and she put several rounds from her handgun into his torso. Hopefully, the police will arrive shortly."

Sirens could be heard in the distance and the music, which had stopped, started up again. The camera turned back around as the trucks began moving; the Cinco de Mayo parade was back in gear. The floats lined the street, people seemed to be enjoying themselves. The horrifying scene at the Piggly Wiggly was quickly forgotten.

Another bloodcurdling scream came from behind the camera, and again it spun. Police cars and an ambulance had gathered in front of the grocery store; suddenly another naked man launched himself at one of the officers. Three other officers had pistols trained on the crazy attacker. Screaming at him to "drop to the ground!" did absolutely nothing, and he charged directly at them. What seemed like dozens of rounds riddled his body, flinging him backwards. The filthy, crazed man sank to the ground, red pooling beneath him.

The reporter mumbled something to the cameraman, but before he could turn around, another insane, nude, screaming person broke from the trees behind the store.

The camera focused on the action as yet another came from the woods. Two more. Another. Now dozens of frenzied, naked, blue individuals rushed into the parking lot. Sirens blared from across the island as emergency vehicles rushed to the scene.

The bright sun seemed to bother the madmen. As they emerged from the cover of the woods, they squinted and covered their eyes, which, the reporter noted, appeared yellow. None attempted to enter the Piggly Wiggly, but were happy to attack fleeing customers as they tried to escape to their cars.

With the camera still watching the violence across the street, the reporter clicked his microphone on and began speaking from off-screen. "This is Clark Carson reporting live from Guntersville. We are at the Cinco de Mayo parade watching an unbelievable scene unfold across the street."

Police officers were emptying magazines as naked people hurled themselves at anyone within reach.

Bullets were flying. As the melee grew, it was hard to tell if citizens were falling from attack or had been taken by crossfire. The yellow-eyed lunatics were winning, at least in their minds; especially when "winning" meant getting a bite of people meat.

Zombies On A Plane

They would jump on a victim, bring their teeth down on exposed flesh, tear out a chunk, and then move on to their next target.

None of the victims were killed outright. Each rose slowly and wandered to their cars or into the store, dazed by the attack. Finally, there were no more unbitten people left in the large parking lot, so the crazies honed in on the large crowd which stood fixated on the scene a few hundred yards away. The cameraman started backing up when the nut cases began coming straight for the Cinco de Mayo parade. A few of the brave spectators came from behind the cameraman to send pistol rounds at the rushing attackers, but within seconds, the bluish lunatics were among the crowd, biting everyone in sight.

Clark Carson could be heard babbling as he started moving about. "Holy shit! They are...they're just fucking biting people!" The camera would catch glimpses of the occasional soul bold or stupid enough to put up a fight; most just tried to flee. The entire crowd was panicking; screaming and crying becoming one chaotic noise. "Fuck this!" The cameraman shouted and dropped his camera before running. It lay on its side, facing the grocery store–a nearly uncountable herd of nude, yellow-eyed, screaming cannibals were covering the screen.

The reporter picked up the camera and held it in his left hand, facing behind him. He started running like his life depended on it. And it did. Reporting the news to the end, he described what he saw as he ran.

"This is Clark Carson reporting live from Guntersville. The Cinco de Mayo parade was disrupted by naked terrorists attacking everyone they could catch." He was staying on the road, almost to the river bridge. His shoes could be heard thudding on the pavement over screams of terror.

Blue flashers leapt onto anyone slow enough to be overtaken by the rushing tide. Like completely wild animals, the crazies threw themselves at oncoming vehicles, occasionally smashing through windshields and fighting with drivers. Carson, still bouncing the camera along, began going uphill with the bridge. Three lunatics noticed the lone man heading over the bridge. They stopped chasing the dog that was not having any part of this shitfest and turned their attention to the tiring runner.

Bare feet smacking against pavement is a very distinct sound; especially when it is the one thing a person dreads hearing. Clark quickly glanced back. "Motherfucker!" His pace picked up considerably as he neared the top of the southbound lanes of the bridge, but he was winded.

Zombies On A Plane

He was sure going down would be easier; it would also be easier for the vicious cannibals behind him.

He began crying as his feet started impacting concrete rather than asphalt. As he crested the hill, the loonies were nearly on him.

Less than a dozen yards away and screaming, it was easy to see their dangling genitals, yellow eyes, and bloodstained mouths. Clark Carson knew there was no escape. No miracle. The camera hung loosely in his hand, filming his attackers below the knee. "Mama, I–" The cry for his mother was cut short. The leading monster dove at his back and knocked the camera to the ground. One of the insane naked people planted a foot on the top of the lens, ending Clark Carson's live report from Guntersville the day the zombies came to TOWN.

Javan Bonds

1

Mo Journal Entry 1

I AM CURRENTLY on a plane that will soon be landing in Birmingham, Alabama–if the pilot does not plow us into a mountain. I figured I should introduce myself and my companions just in case you have discovered this journal in the ruins of Birmingham beside either a pile of bones or clothes. You guessed it, if this is the first of my journals you are reading, I'm dead or blue.

My name is Mo Collins, I'm twenty-nine, and I'm pretty average–or at least I was, before Smokes dubbed me The Hero of our little horror show. Please find Guntersville Island in Marshall County, Alabama and give this notebook to the interim mayor, my father, Randy Collins. By the way, yes, I am a dude. And thanks for not immediately thinking of the chick from *Mad TV*.

The pilot of this single engine plane is Marlon "Smokes" Williamson, whom I have dubbed The Oracle because apparently, he knows every possible outcome in this screenplay my life seems to be following.

Javan Bonds

The only other passenger is The Expert, Captain Petunia "Hammer" Sledge. She's one of those former military bad asses, eyepatch and all that has killed more people than I've ever even met and she is insanely delusional.

She thinks all the peevies, (our word for the plague victims, who are basically zombies), are simply communists that need to be eliminated. I feel so safe surrounding myself with an extremely over-weight version of Chris Tucker and the one eyed lunatic sister of Kathy Bates. How did Hammer lose her eye? I don't have the balls to ask her.

Actually, I don't suppose it's too bad; I've been around them both for close to a month and so far so good. We met right after May 1, the initial day the infection broke in America. Somehow I've avoided dying in a grotesque fashion, or any fashion, I guess.

Anyway, Smokes is the sole reason I am where I am right now and why everything has played out like it has since our meeting. I have become, and will remain, a firm believer in his gospel–at least until I have the smallest reason to doubt. This nutty professor has introduced and continues to introduce me to all the characters I'm supposed to meet.

Zombies On A Plane

Back in Guntersville, where our adventures started, there is The Tech, The Old Friend, The Love Interest, The Man of God, The Medicine Man...what's left of The Similar, and a shitload of insignificant characters who started flocking to the island once we made it an actual island. We are on our way to Birmingham to find the second part of The Reasons (all heroes need quests, reasons to go, reasons to stay), my brother, Ezekiel "Easy" Collins, and maybe come across a few other inevitables on our trip to fill out our character list. The first installment of The Reasons was addressed in my first two journals when I rescued my parents and Sarah Ogle, the woman I've been madly in love with for a decade, from The Villain, a rogue, ironfisted unit of former US military troops led, to my amusement, by a Cpt. Bobbitt. I'm hoping we'll find Easy alive in his dorm room so we can turn around and be home before the sun goes down, when the fucking nocturnal peevies start coming out.

But knowing my damn luck, something will go horribly wrong and we'll be stuck down here for a week, won't find anything more than his body, and will barely make it back after losing a few appendages or a main protagonist. Maybe I can get Smokes to have a conversation with The Screenwriter; he should give me a break for ONCE.

Javan Bonds

2

Chief Engineer Gene Stanley's Log 1

If you found Mo's first journal, you may know me as The Tech. Mo told me about his writings, his inspiration (plus a list of books to read if we happen to scavenge them), and I agree that someone should chronicle current events. He explained the reason he titled his journals, for the name of his replica caravel, *The Viva Ancora*, or the *Cora*, as we call her.

Though our writing styles are as different as Jedi and Sith, our missions are as similar as Romulan and Vulcan genetics, so I hope my increased vernacular does not bore you any more than the new *Godzilla* probably did. As a child, I devoured *Star Trek*, *Star Wars*, *Battlestar Galactica*, classic science fiction, and everything since then about aliens, robots, or outer space.

Javan Bonds

Excelsior Comics and Collectables, the shop I own and manage, has recently become my home though I have always spent a fair amount of time there. It has complete solar electrical independence, and it puts me closer to Georgia, Daniel Daniels' distraught widow, who, so far, just seems to need a friend. The Admiral (Mo calls her The Expert, Captain Sledge), and the all-knowing-all-seeing token black guy–titled The Oracle, Marlon "Smokes" Williamson have journeyed with Mo by plane to Birmingham, on a quest to rescue Mo's brother. The remainder of the primary group has chosen to stay in Guntersville to continue developing our thriving island community. I'm monitoring their radio communication; maybe now I will finally be able to catch up on *Lost*. The away team is reportedly closing on Birmingham International Airport and will be landing soon. Though I have not been in direct audio contact with the travelers, Mayor Randy Collins, Mo's dad, has been in nearly constant communication with the trio. I hope they are safe and everything works out within an hour like most adventures involving the *Enterprise*. Oh no…I just realized: Smokes is wearing a red SHIRT!

3

Mo Journal Entry 2

REMEMBER THAT FLYOVER of New York City in *I Am Legend,* after the end of the world, where there's nothing moving at all? This was like that. I mean, I've been up here before; I went to the occasional local air shows as a kid and got to ride in some of the small planes. Marshall County, Alabama doesn't have ten million residents, but you could see traffic on the highway and cows in the pastures. Now, absolutely nothing; not a single sign of life anywhere. No cars moving, no banners on top of buildings that read "alive inside" or "help us" or anything. This has been one boring plane ride. I want a refund.

"Are we there yet?"

"Cracka, we be on da ground if we was. Where we gonna land dis thang anyway?"

"I figured the airport. I reckon you don't need much runway; it's not like you'll have to coordinate with the FAA."

I knew Birmingham's international airport was fairly large, though I had never actually been in the airport. I had driven past it several times and was pretty sure we'd have room even if the runways were cluttered and if, for some strange reason, the airport was inaccessible, I was fairly certain we could find a stretch of empty highway on which to land.

The Oracle looked grim as he spoke, "I don't know watchoo thankin' white bread, Beavas ain't made fo nuffin but wata."

It's a good thing I don't have a weak stomach. "You have to be shitting me."

Smokes nearly fell out of his seat with an explosion of laughter. "Hells yeah dawg! I's fuckin wichoo! Alex gots custom wheels built in da floats."

I looked at him suspiciously, smirking at the name he had dubbed the plane. He continued, "I lay on da dock and checked all up inside fo wheels afo we lef!"

Zombies On A Plane

I was hesitantly satisfied, still a little uncomfortable. He looked at me like I was an evil heretic. "Scats, I could land dis shit in a swimmin' pool if I had to, fo sho."

I was incredulous. "I'd rather you not when there's a perfectly good fucking airport with runways right below us. That would be an embarrassing way to die."

The Oracle simply shrugged his shoulders in acceptance. "As you wish, cracka."

Look, I survived the zombie apocalypse. Next I held together survivors to make our post-Armageddon life easier. I saved the woman I love and my parents, who were The Reasons, from imminent decimation by The Villain, an insane para military band. After that, I turned Guntersville *peninsula* into an actual island, which became a sanctuary for any survivor that asked for refuge. There was no way I was going out by swimming pool? I would be so pissed that I would kill Smokes again!

I had discussed with my father that I would keep my radio on at least for the plane trip. You know, in case I had to give a quick farewell as we tumbled to earth. The radio buzzed. "Mo. This is Logan. You copy?"

"Yeah, Gene. What's up?"

"Ran across any blunatics yet?" His smile could be heard through the radio.

"'Blunatics?'" I had to ask. That was a new one. I half guessed he was using that word to refer to peevies. I wanted to say, "Yes, Gene we've been in the air for twenty fucking minutes. Of course we've had clashes with hordes of revenants," but I let him have his moment.

He sounded back. "Combination of 'blue' and 'lunatics,' get it?"

I played dumb for him. "I'm talking about the zombies. Lucas-esque, don't you think?"

"Uh, yeah, Gene…pretty cool, man." Thanks for the verification. Does everyone think I'm a retard? I exhaled. "Nothing yet, still in the plane." I wanted to add "dumbass" but remained civil. "When we touchdown, I'll let you know if we run into any 'blunatics.'" That's actually a pretty good one. I think I'm going to start using it.

Zombies On A Plane

After several minutes, The Oracle had seemingly forgotten all about our previous conversation. He rocked in his seat and said, "I need to talk to a man 'bout a dawg."

An older line, but not unheard of. He needed to pee.

I felt like my mother scolding a petulant child. "We were at the *Cora* just a few minutes ago! Why didn't you go before we left?"

He cut his eyes at me and wheezed as he rocked back and forth. I continued, "You'll just have to wait until we land, we can't pull over."

He howled in pain. "Mufucka, I's 'bout to go R. Kelly on yo ass!"

I looked around for some type of receptacle; I pulled an empty Mountain Dew bottle from under the seat. I lifted it and offered it to him as he looked over with disgust. "Fuck you cracka, I'm black!"

I was a bit offended. "So? I use Coke bottles all the time!"

If you're a guy, you know exactly what I'm thinking. We've all pissed in bottles rather than stop the car; Big Gulp in, Big Gulp out. I almost had a *Dumb and Dumber* moment in high school when my mom decided to take a full Mountain Dew bottle from my passenger seat and stick it in the fridge. She was probably checking my car to make sure I didn't have any used condoms or marijuana cigarettes in there. That incident taught me to always smell before consuming.

"I don't give a fuck if you can stick yo tiny white pecker in–"

"No! Just–for God's sake–be a good aim!"

He looked at me again as if I had no idea what I was talking about and pushed the proffered Mountain Dew bottle back in my direction. I angrily said, "Fine, just fucking piss your pants, I don't give a shit!"

My over-weight friend reached down to his left and lifted an empty thirty-two ounce styrofoam cup, grinning. "DIS how we do it mufucka. Turn yo head or da beauty of it might make ya gay."

Zombies On A Plane

I turned my head for my own obvious reasons as he made splashing sounds and noises I'd only heard during pornos. In between moans, he continued regaling me with details of his amazing member. I was too busy looking below to pay attention to his ramblings; the city of Birmingham had just come into view.

I gestured for him to do a quick flyover of the dead city, hoping to see movement or any signs of life. I held out hope that we would discover the two sexiest fat men alive, Rick and Bubba, patrolling the streets of the lifeless metropolis and keeping order. Nothing. I was still optimistic; maybe we just needed to drive by the radio station after we landed, perhaps they were somehow still doing broadcasts. I made a mental note to scan through the stations and listen for Bill "Bubba" Bussey doing a "phone-trolls" or screaming "Stay In It". Sorry, non-Alabamans…I probably left y'all behind there.

"Dat smell just like bologna fo some reason." The Oracle quoted Robert Downey Jr. from *Tropic Thunder* while snapping the lid back onto the cup.

I honestly don't know why I did it, but I sniffed and nodded in agreement; an animal instinct, I suppose.

Hammer, in the back, contemplating our mission parameters, leaned forward and rang in her agreement, scaring the holy hell out of me. I had almost forgotten she'd tagged along, she'd been so quiet.

As we circled back in the direction of the airport, The Oracle nearly passed out with joy. "Lordy mercy child! Da land of milk and honey!"

Before I could even find what he saw, he veered the plane to the right and for a horrifying nano-second I thought he was going to a nose-dive *Alex* into the ground.

We leveled off and Smokes didn't appear to notice my life streaking before my eyes. I swallowed the shrill scream and calmly asked, "What'd you do that for? We don't need to put Hammer's heart under extra stress." I settled myself and looked very annoyed at him, cleverly deflecting my own terror.

As if that was a completely routine maneuver, the seer turned for what seemed like an unsafe length of time while flying a plane.

"Just a course correction, mufucka."

I raised an eyebrow. "To?"

Zombies On A Plane

He pointed down to a pile up on the interstate. I was expecting to see a Hostess truck, immediately realizing the scene below was just like one in *Zombieland*. It would be pretty cool to run into Woody Harrelson, though. It goes without saying that this might be the most important find of Smokes's life: a Newport eighteen wheeler. I wasn't sure how we would transport a tractor-trailer full of cigarettes, but I'm sure The Oracle would cross that bridge when we got there.

I looked up, taking a breath to ask where we would land but he answered the question on my lips by pointing out the left window.

There was a completely clean stretch of interstate at least the length of a football field only a few hundred yards from our intended destination. That had to be more than luck!

I cut my eyes at him, still not completely trusting that we had landing gear. "That's not water."

"I done told you dick wrangler, we got wheels."

The Oracle landed smoothly on our open four lane runway. Yet again, I am proven to be faithful depending on the weather. It's not that I want to doubt his words, I just have a hard time accepting that which I cannot touch, see, or smell.

Once the plane was barely crawling, Smokes slung his door open, flung himself out, and was running at the speed of one of those skinny African dudes at the Olympics. I wasn't sure how it was possible for him, but I was even more surprised he was able to stop without falling over.

He stood at the doors, smiling like a kid on Christmas as his passengers walked up behind him.

He drew his shotgun which alerted the two of us to draw weapons as well. He deftly jumped onto the back bumper of the tractor trailer and shot the lock for the sliding door. I immediately felt stupid for expecting any kind of peevie incursion during the middle of the day. But as he opened the door to reveal cavernous black, I realized why we had drawn our guns.

It just didn't seem worth risking my life to get a fix for a habit I no longer partook of. "I ain't going in–"

He raised a hand to silence me. "Don't care, mufucka." And he was gone. He raced into the gaping maw of assured death before I could say another word.

Zombies On A Plane

Hammer and I stood staring into the empty blackness for a moment, stupefied and expecting to hear The Oracle's death throes as he was mauled. When we were able to close our jaws, she broke a glow stick and tossed it into the abyss. With the blackness now bathed in a weird green glow, we watched a scene from a classic martial arts movie featuring Fat Albert as the hero.

Smokes ran at a peevie that was already running at him, he drew a knife as he charged at the monster and plunged the serrated blade into the top of its left shoulder while it was in midair. It felt like *The Matrix;* things impossibly stopped as he raised his shotgun to the creature's head and let loose a blast of buckshot.

As it fell, The Oracle yanked his bloody blade free before straightening his arm and launching the dagger at another enemy coming towards him from somewhere off screen. The blade lodged in this one's throat, sending it to the floor to choke to death on its own blood.

What the fuck? Zombies attacking one at a time? Of course, none of them were wearing shirts, I was expecting his final opponent to walk up slowly, say a few words overlaid by an American narrator, bow, and engage in martial combat to the death.

It was unbelievable to see McDonald's number one customer spin like a ballerina and blow holes through his attackers.

There were five naked people dead, *really* dead, on the floor at his feet and The Oracle looked completely untouched. The only way I knew that had even just fucking happened was the fact that he was drenched in sweat. I take that back, Smokes is always covered in sweat and should carry one of those old man handkerchiefs. If The Expert had not been staring with the same incredulous amazement, I would have assumed I had merely imagined the epic fight scene.

The tractor-trailer was basically empty of tobacco; we were able to see nothing but empty shelves. Our token prophet walked to the corner, picked something up with reverence, and carried out a box of at least a dozen cartons of Newport Unfiltered.

He smiled, the victorious champion. "Told you mufucka. I gots what I come fo."

If I were still dipping, would I have reacted the same to the site of a US Smokeless Tobacco truck? This truck must have just made its last stop, having basically no merchandise on board. He could have gotten himself killed for just a few cancer sticks!

Zombies On A Plane

How did he know where to find the insignificant amount of tobacco in the truck? Is he a nicotine bloodhound? And how the hell did he pull off that Bruce Lee shit? I swear to God, that fight scene could have been in *300*. Maybe to him, just the possibility of sucking tobacco is like spinach for fucking Popeye.

Even when I was a tobacco user, I don't believe my habit would have compared to his commitment. I asked the man who was trying to set a world record for smoking a cigarette the fastest, "Is that it?"

Hammer had made her way around to the cab and stuck her head out of the door. "Look what I got!"

The Expert was just as good at discovering her poison of choice as The Oracle. I didn't notice her sneaking up there, maybe she has the same teleportation powers as he.

She walked in our direction and raised her left hand. "This was the best idea you've ever had, big boy!" She shook a nearly full pack of Beech Nut chewing tobacco in her nicotine yellowed hand. The late driver was apparently a chewer and not a smoker.

I can empathize. Even if they were offering him free Newports. I've smoked cigarettes, sure, but I will throw a menthol down no matter how hammered I am.

Not only does menthol bring to mind drinking a bottle of gasoline and swallowing a lit match, it's probably just as bad for you.

She raised her right hand as if just remembering a side note. "Oh, and there's this." A beautiful, shiny, straight from the silver screen, Colt 45 1911.

Jesus Christ! The people around me magically find things that make them unbelievably happy while I'm just lucky not to get fucking bit! Well, Smokes could have smashed *Alex* into the ground by now, I guess I can be thankful for something.

"We kind of need to get a move on." I tapped my bare wrist to indicate that time's wasting.

The Oracle clicked his tongue and shot a finger pistol at me. "Fo sho dawg."

The three of us loaded back into the cabin of the single-engine plane and I wondered how long I was going to be able to breathe through the smoke. I wished we could roll the windows down!

Zombies On A Plane

Our Beaver turned and began speeding up to take off. It's funny how we could be only feet away from active peevies and somehow not become blue. But there's always an opportunity we will meet our un-deaths in the next episode. Tune in, same bat time, same bat CHANNEL!

Javan Bonds

4

Mo Journal Entry 3

I GESTURED MY head in the direction of the airport and could see that there would be enough room for us to land. Smokes had told me earlier "I's can land dis shit on half a football field," and there was, miraculously, at least that much runway clear. The fleeing populace obviously didn't make it off the ground because there were not a lot of stalled jets on the tarmac though there were a few that had veered off into the grass.

No details were easily visible of the cityscape from this point; I could see the same tall buildings and the same roads, but no movement. Apparently there had been no massive, city destroying fires; Birmingham looked depressingly peaceful. We closed on our landing strip and started the drop.

Once we had stopped, we decided it would be best to find a working vehicle onsite before making our way to Easy's UAB dormitory. I'm amazed–maybe we have subconsciously learned walking is not the only form of transportation.

I had been to his dorm only once and I don't even remember the reason why–probably when he first moved in or maybe he had been awarded some type of scholarship for awesome people. The one thing that has stuck with me about that apartment was the fact that it was just so clean and perfect, the strong aroma of his cologne permeated everything.

The three of us made our way in the direction of a few airport utility trucks. I was crossing my fingers in hopes that they weren't dead and that the keys were close by. I figured with my luck, each would have at least one dead body rotting and festering in the cab.

My large companion veered to the left as we walked. I asked calmly, "Where the fuck do you think you're going?"

"Listen cracka," he gestured to the airport. "I know dey's a 'Chicken-Fil-A' in dere and I'm a gemme a chicken samwich and some waffle fries."

I wasn't going to ask him what he wanted to drink, we were already in *unforgivable* territory. Was Smokes turning into Hammer now? He couldn't seriously believe any restaurant in there would be open.

Hell, how did he even know if there was a Chick-fil-A in the airport? Was he guessing or had he seen it in one of his visions from the future?

He continued walking away. I shouted to his back, "You do know it will be closed, right?"

"What nigga, you think I's stupid? I used to work at da one in Guntersville, maybe I can get da frya up."

The ridiculousness of his idea dawned now and he stopped and kicked his foot at absolutely nothing. "Shit, I wanna fuckin' chicken samwich!"

He wanted some normalcy and I could relate. "We'll get you one tonight when we get back, I think I'll have one too."

The Oracle began walking back in my direction. I smiled and tacked on, "And a Dr. Pepper, bitch."

By the grace of God or the master direction of The Screenwriter, the first utility truck we inspected had nearly a full tank of gas and a ring of keys resting on the seat. When something like this happens, I see our good fortune as predestined fate and believe the words of The Oracle. I'm faithful–that is until something shitty happens. Then I am back to being mired in doubt.

The three of us squeezed into the truck, Hammer taking the wheel for some reason. Maybe it was because deep down we all feel safer having a driver who's a stickler for traffic laws, or it could just be my lack of initiative, but she always seems to be the one behind the wheel. Following the fifteen mile-per-hour posted speed limit, we cautiously made our way to the end of the parking lot where we passed an empty tollbooth with blood smeared across the inside of the cracked service window.

I'd never seen this airport when it was not busy and I breathed a sigh of relief after getting off their property; it was eerie as hell. I can't really describe the feeling of being near a place that used to be bustling with activity but is now deathly quiet. It had a *Langoliers* creepiness to it.

"Lady, da lights ain't workin'! Why da hell is you turnin' da blinker on?"

After the first few attempts, I realized that it was pointless to argue with The Expert about her driving etiquette; these battles were as unproductive as arguments revolving around race with Smokes. I have learned to sit back quietly and take it most of the time while The Oracle had to bitch about everything.

There's nothing to be gained from debating with crazy people–Hammer, that is–I'm not saying black people are crazy.

See? I don't even need help making myself sound like a Grand Wizard.

"Just because the lights are off doesn't mean that I won't get a ticket." she stated adamantly as if a paddy wagon was waiting just around the corner.

He shook his head, unable to understand her caution since this was probably the only automobile moving south of Guntersville. "But dey ain't no otha cars on da road!"

I wanted to correct him because there actually were cars on the road, they were just stopped or wrecked. I was wise enough to remain quiet. Their bickering continued for a few more blocks of coming to complete stops and signaling before turning. The Expert made cautious, wide arcs around the stalls and the few fender benders we encountered. I briefly wondered if she recognized that these vehicles were dead. Maybe she had created some other reason there were empty automobiles in the middle of normally busy streets in a normally busy city. Somewhere in her unstable mind, we were still traveling in traffic and were still beholden to its rules.

Birmingham felt a lot like Guntersville directly after May Day. There were no craters from huge explosions, grotesque leftovers of obvious mutilations, no burning buildings or military presence, nothing to indicate The End of the World. There was just peevie shit splattered copiously and the eerie absence of bird chirping. If you were blind and not able to smell the gut wrenching excrement surrounding you, you might think this was just a really peaceful day.

If I think about it too long, I start to wonder if maybe we are just three crazy people traveling through Alabama cities during a lull in activity. If I had not spent the past month running away from blue nudists and seeing a group of bad guys destroy my hometown while using zombie guard dogs, I might feel right in thinking we are escaped mental patients, good pals that murdered a state representative, stole his plane, then landed illegally at an international airport. I'd have to be pretty messed up, but I guess it could happen.

We came to the UAB dormitory building where my brother roomed. I was almost certain Easy was inside and just waiting for his older sibling to rescue him. You know, because I'm the badass of the Collins' offspring.

I exclaimed, "Just park here–right here! Right on the street and we can use the stairs!"

Zombies On A Plane

"Chill dawg, ain't no need in gettin' excited."

I was somewhat worried Hammer would have made an attempt to enter the parking deck attached to the building prior to my exclamation and was acting preemptively. That would have been the complete opposite of fucking enjoyable, so I had a pretty damn good reason to get excited. I'm surprised the parking deck scene from *Dawn of the Dead* didn't flashed through his mind; then again, plenty of nasty shit goes down on abandoned streets, too.

The other two in this trio had obviously forgotten the feral ghouls that are hiding in almost every shadow. I know that makes me sound a little bit paranoid, but I really don't give a shit. I understand the odds, but I'd rather not chance running into a nocturnal cannibal lurking in a darkened corner and possibly ending up blue and naked. I've seen this film; it doesn't end well for everyone.

Thankfully, the parallel parking spots in front of the building were open. After squaring the truck perfectly, The Expert killed the engine and signaled we were safe to unbuckle our seat belts.

The building's glass front doors were unlocked and we entered with no obvious worries. I could've sworn I detected a hint of bleach or some type of cleaning solution in the air. Most of the stairwell was brightly lit by an almost seamless window that stretched the entire height of the building. Actually, I guess I was wrong about that window being seamless. Four stories up we came to a hallway bathed in nearly complete blackness. There were cracked open doors on the outer-side spilling the faintest amount of light.

"Is this a joke, God?" I looked back down from the heavens before asking my compatriots. "Okay, who wants to go through first?"

"You white; you always gets ta go first, cracka. How you like it?"

"What the hell does that mean? She's as white as I am!" I gestured to Hammer. "And what about 'ladies first?'" Hammer shrugged. I resigned myself to my fate and broke a glow stick. "I'll run the gauntlet but cover my ass. Take out any that chase."

It goes without saying that the Expert is a phenomenal shot compared to me so I was more than willing to trust her accuracy. I can shoot; I'm just not a super soldier that can hit a bull's-eye with a pistol at nine hundred yards. Her mastery could not be contested.

Zombies On A Plane

The idea of just using a flash bang had crossed my mind, but I really didn't want to ring the dinner bell for every peevie in the city.

The husky seer dropped to a knee and aimed down the pitch corridor. "I got yo back dawg."

Not you, dumbass." I slapped my forehead. "You are holding a shotgun!"

He held his gun away from him and looked at it with a cocked eyebrow. As if to say, "No shit, cracka."

I'm from rural Alabama, I have put more shells through shotguns throughout my life than I can count. Most were not what you'd call tight shots. Would you feel safe being anywhere but behind a shotgun when it sprays pellets everywhere?

Until this moment, I had assumed The Oracle had shared similar experiences during his childhood. I simply shook my head. "Get the fuck up and let Hammer take your position."

He rose, shrugged his shoulders as he walked away. He let me know, "Whateva cracka, it yo funeral."

He just couldn't understand how I could trust a Specter with genetically enhanced accuracy more than a cartoon character with ADD. Would you prefer Agent 86 from *Get Smart*, or *Hitman's* Agent 47 firing high-powered rounds in the general direction of your clumsy ass?

She got into position and held up three fingers. "On the count of three." She dropped one finger. "One–"

"Whoa! How are you going to do it?"

She looked at me stupidly. I clarified, "One, two, go on three?" I gestured for her to let me continue. "Or one, two, three, go?"

This is a valid question. That extra half-second could mean the difference of a piece of lead in my ass. She shook her head sadly the same way I did earlier and said, "Ready–"

She tightened her grip on her rifle. "Set–"

Given no time to think, I simply started moving and passed her the instant she barked, "Go!"

Zombies On A Plane

I ran in a zigzag pattern, praying the expert shot straight. When nothing jumped out of the doors, I began to wonder if this floor even contained any dorm rooms. I've seen Bradley's monkey, Mary, turn knobs to open doors. Peevies had started to seem pretty intelligent, for ravenous animals, and I'm not going to believe the ones I saw open doors at the Best Western were oddities. Until I see proof otherwise, I'm going to assume every one of the fuckers can lock-pick advanced difficulty doors with nothing more than a bobby pin and a screwdriver like they do in *Fallout*. Over halfway down the hallway, at the apex of one of my zigs, the one door that opened outwardly, collided with my face, and the back of my head collided with the FLOOR.

Javan Bonds

5

Mo Journal Entry 4

Prophecy from *The Book of Smokes*

The Loner is a character that will be discovered secluded from the rest of the pre-and/or post-apocalyptic world and may be completely unaware that the dead walk. Regardless of seclusion or ignorance, the monsters do not bother this protagonist often. This inevitable character may be initially reluctant to join with the main protagonists, having been fine on his or her own, but will ultimately find or invent a role among the group.

"Does he do that a lot?" I heard an unfamiliar voice ask as I snapped back into consciousness.

"Yeah, he has a tendency to faint pretty easy."

Well fuck you too, Hammer. Receiving serious head trauma and being knocked unconscious is not the same thing as fainting!

Javan Bonds

I wasn't active in sports during high school, but I had been rendered unconscious by physical blows on more than one occasion throughout my life; not to mention nearly cracking my skull in a gas station just a few days ago. That episode with the cans rolling across the mini-mart floor flashed across my mind as she insinuated to this stranger that I was a weakling.

I was unable to think of any reasonable defense. I shouted, "I didn't faint! Getting hit in the head is different! How long was I out anyway?"

Smokes shrugged. "You was still layin' on da flo, sleepin' long nuff fo us to get a new friend."

What the hell does that mean? I looked over to where the seer was nodding.

An older black man in a janitor's uniform greeted me. "I know you're Mo; I'm Tychus, Tychus Jones."

I blinked, not sure if my recent brain injury was affecting my perception. I was looking at the winner of the Morgan Freeman look alike contest who clearly wasn't a fan of *StarCraft*.

"Where's Jim Raynor?" I asked as I envisioned the janitor in a set of Gene's power armor.

I'm fairly sure he wasn't playing along and I'm betting we weren't thinking about the same person. He stated flatly, "I haven't seen that man in years and I believe he died long before these blue monsters came along."

He raised a questioning eyebrow to ask how I knew his old friend, but I asked first, "Do you live here?"

I was thinking that this guy could be part of my brother's surviving tribe, another group that would come to be labeled as The Similar. I would nod my head as he told me of how Easy had been governing their community as a perfect benefactor; of how they are actually better off now because of my God-sent brother than they would have been with some weak mortal controlling the community.

But Tychus shot down my dreams like he would a Zerg. "Yep, just me and an old Adjutant. I've been working here thirty years; so far this building has been pretty safe. There were a few students here, but they said they heard something about some kind of sanctuary or something a few miles away and left a couple of weeks ago. And no, I haven't heard from them since they left."

"Who's the adjutant?" I asked. I know I'm not the only one that immediately thought of the computer with the same name from the video game.

"Adjutant is my cat."

"So, just you then? There's no infected hiding in these rooms?"

"Not last time I checked; I've been all over the building."

"And you just leave the doors unlocked? I'm pretty sure they can open those."

"They sure can. But when you came in through the lobby, didn't you smell the cleaning solution? Seems they don't like that, so I mop the floors every day, just like I always have. Keeps them out and keeps me occupied." I nearly laughed at that, thinking of the shit covered cannibals turning their noses up at something that didn't reek.

So bleach or Pine Sol, or whatever, was a peevie repellent? I would have to remember to test that out. Maybe it was chlorine or some lemony freshness in the cleaning solution.

Tychus continued and chuckled as he spoke. "Plus it might be just me. I don't guess they like old, chewy jerky," he said, gesturing down to his leathery and bony frame.

I think all of The Oracle's talk about me being The Hero has built up some type of classic savior complex in my mind. "You should come with us. Even if we don't find this sanctuary you were talking about, we live on an island that is peevie-free. My home is the *Viva Ancora*, but there are plenty of houses you can live in."

"I was getting kind of so much quiet; I know this is a safe place but I miss company. I'll likely take you up on that offer."

He added, "'Peevies?'"

I grinned. "That's our name for the zombies."

I had always just figured everyone was calling them peevies since it was a term used quite often on the news immediately following the outbreak. In *The Walking Dead*, everyone automatically understands the zombies are referred to as "walkers." I'm just hoping this is not going to be one of those things I have to explain to every newcomer I encounter like I do when it comes to the damn boat.

I was about to speak again when he brought up another question. "Are there any cows on your island? I'd kill for a steak."

"Fo sho, homey," Smokes answered. "An I gots nuff weed to bake a cake wit."

The janitor nodded with understanding and I was a bit taken aback; senior citizens and illegal drugs have never been connected in my mind. Apparently, everyone else understood that to be a good amount, but I don't believe I'd ever heard the saying Smokes just used.

What the hell is wrong with me? When did I become such a generous saint? Just over a month ago, I guarantee you I would never have offered a free plane ticket to a stranger and now I feel duty-bound to help everyone? I blame Smokes. If this kept up we would have to run shuttle flights.

Our new friend had no clue where the students had gone and I decided to go check Easy's dorm room for any clues.

When I entered the spotless and pristine apartment, I noticed on the vanity a piece of paper directed to "Whom It May Concern," in my brother's handwriting.

In his perfect calligraphy he wrote that he and several other students were leaving for a state prison in Jefferson County that they had been told was being used as a safe zone by (at least) the local government.

Zombies On A Plane

His letter was dated and thankfully included a hand-drawn map directing the reader to that location.

Before leaving my bodybuilder brother's room to give the map to our pilot, I made sure to stuff a few protein bars in my pocket. It was getting late in the afternoon, I was not holding out hope we would be home before sundown and guessed we would be spending the night in the plane once we landed near this prison–lucky us. We might need something to tide us over, I was sure the Oracle would.

Oh, and yes, I had just told the janitor the *Viva Ancora* was my "home." It's sad really.

I was kind of disappointed to exit the dorm building without my brother to show for it, just another miserable failure of Mo Collins. Maybe I could surprise him by showing up at this prison/fortress and take him home tomorrow, where he will be bathed in gratitude for returning. His presence will automatically increase morale and general happiness of the community.

They will no doubt build statues dedicated to the manly manliness of Easy and there will be several books written about him. I can see these books being sold in the distant future to teenage girls who will name their children Ezekiel. These New York Times bestsellers will be on the bookshelves beside *The Book of Smokes*, scriptures that will be nearly as popular as the Bible. I guess living The Gospel According to Smokes has led me to believe that just as my parents, Easy is alive and well, and not in desperate need of my assistance.

We made it back to the airport and our ride, *Alex*, with surprisingly no interesting conversation from The Oracle. There were only introductions and brief pleasantries between The Expert and our newly recruited follower.

I turned to the prophet as we walked down the runway. "I reckon we just found The Loner."

"No shit Watson. You gots a learnt teacha!"

The plane ride was relatively short. It seemed after only a few seconds in the air Smokes exclaimed, "Oh shit cracka!"

I sat up excitedly. "What's wrong?"

Zombies On A Plane

"Dat's it! He pointed down to a large, fenced in compound up a creek–hopefully not literally–a few miles from a lake.

Why the hell would you do that? If you are an amateur flying a small plane with absolutely no radio access to any sort of assistance, don't be so damned excitable: I'm not even going to list the possibilities of catastrophic failures he could've been screaming about.

"Y"all wanna go fo da lake er da riva?"

"Just go for the damn lake! it's wide open and there's nothing to hit. We can sleep in the plane and drive up the creek in a boat or something in the morning."

"You questioni' my pilotin' skills, cracka?"

I wasn't going to beat around the bush. I had been willing to get in the plane with him, but I prefer not to take any more risks than absolutely necessary. "Yes. I am."

Maybe he put himself in my shoes, realizing that I'd had less than an hour of proof that he knew how to fly a plane any better than I did. He simply shrugged before gently landing in the middle of the lake.

I had never been through this part of the state; there was this secluded lake, the fortified prison a few miles away, and absolutely nothing but trees in every direction for what seemed like millions of miles. Even before the zombie apocalypse, you wouldn't really have been able to tell there was anyone alive in this area. If I had been one of those crazy hermit survivalists this would have been a great place to build my bunker.

The Loner asked a question out of nowhere. "Did you say something about the *"Viva Ancora"* earlier?"

Oh dear God, even this janitor, all the way out here, who doesn't really seem like the type of person that would be interested in pointless shit, asks about the damn boat.

I rolled my eyes, as I do every time this is asked. "Yes."

"The pirate ship? You live on it?"

I pinched the bridge of my nose and realized this was going to be just as painful as every other time. "Yes."

Zombies On A Plane

The same exact tirade of questions was asked, ended by the customary, "Well, I would really like to get a tour."

I think I'm being punished for being a shallow jackass. A pandemic sweeps across the world and kills everyone that the characters in this zombie movie knows and loves, but these idiots are all more concerned with hitting an elementary school field trip destination than finding friends or family. I've always hated being asked about the boat, and maybe I've never had a reason before. But now, I think it's safe to say there might be something more important to care about. Perhaps people are just trying to keep their minds off the fact that they have lost everything; maybe I'm being too much of an asshole. Big surprise.

A few minutes later when Hammer and Tychus (with Adjutant curled up next to him) were sound asleep in the back and I was finishing up my journal entry, Smokes whispered, "Shit, homeslice. 'Erbody ask you the same damn thang?"

Yes, yes they DO.

Javan Bonds

Interlude 1

WE SAT IN the darkening plane on the still water, chatting occasionally as we waited to receive a radio transmission.

It finally came. "Mo, this is Gray Fox. Do you copy?"

I sighed. "Yeah, Daddy, I got you."

My father graciously chose to skip the damn radio lingo and just conversed. "This is our first long-range communication. Gene set up a solar charger on the transmitter in the fire station at the top of the mountain, so we'll be able to communicate any time."

Holy shit, Gene! How many solar panels do you have? Although we could now get with one another at any time, but we decided to keep our debriefings to just after sunset every day.

I could tell he was itching for a report about his favorite son, so I gave him one. "Easy left a note in his dorm with a map to Joseph A. Davidson Correctional Facility which is about an hour from Birmingham. We are sitting in the nearby lake now."

"Your brother's in prison?"

I almost laughed. Yeah, Daddy. The officers allowed him to leave a note for friends before they carted him off. "Well not really. This prison is supposed to be some kind of sanctuary."

I got my curiosity from my father, so I drew out my information until I was sure it was painful. I could almost hear his silent screams for more. Finally I continued. "I haven't seen him yet, but we'll be headed that way first thing tomorrow."

I could feel the tension ease from over the radio. "Anything new on your end?" Dammit, I just remembered that I had not even mentioned our new compatriot. I guess Daddy will meet him when we show up.

Zombies On A Plane

He came back, "After Gene set up that transmitter at the firehouse this morning, he and a few others started rigging up gas powered generators all over the island. Those will last us a while, but we are still looking for somebody to work the dam."

What the fuck? Almost everyone on the island has been without power for weeks and the moment I leave they decide to power everything?

I mean yeah, the *Cora* has been energized throughout the zombie apocalypse, first with propane and then with The Tech's solar panels, meaning that I've been able to get hot showers, but I'm still going to bitch. I'm sure there has to be a fucking barber left alive and I've been in serious need of a haircut with an electric razor; my flattop is getting pretty shaggy.

I was too incredulous to speak. He supplied, "Oh, and the birds are back." He continued with what I was just about to say, "Things just seem to happen when you leave."

No shit. My traveling companions include a delusional senior that believes keeping her pristine driving record untarnished trumps avoiding becoming blue and naked.

The other is the reason McDonald's sold 1 million hamburgers; he also received an early release of the script to my life but refuses to let me in on what is going to happen. Is it any wonder I don't particularly enjoy traveling? I'm sleeping on a water plane in the middle of a lake with water the only thing between me and becoming a carnivorous animal with no more sphincter control than The Old Friend's monkey. I always end up in situations like this and it really doesn't leave me itching to vacation very often.

As I conversed with my dad, I looked out the window to watch a couple of zombie children wrestling before an undead audience on the beach. They gnawed on each other–amazingly, not drawing blood. They rolled and stirred up dust in the moonlight before one stood over the other, breathing heavy–the obvious victor.

The older walkers began chattering and seemed to congratulate the winner of this tiny battle. This was another one of those "that's too-human moments" we had witnessed exhibited by the monsters. Seeing expressions of emotion, even apparent love from these creatures, would only make it harder to kill them when the time came. The disgusting scenes of disemboweled dogs and baby food diarrhea would not be able to mask that these things were once people.

Zombies On A Plane

Even shit-covered, naked, retarded cannibals can be affectionate and this display could be compared to any young children wrestling in the back yard in front of their parents. This will make me hesitate to pull the trigger and that might be my end.

I couldn't even begin to speculate as to the why avian flocks decided to return within hours of my leaving and asked my dad what came to mind: "Just on the island or you mean everywhere?"

"I'm not sure yet, I just know that they are on the island now."

I swear to God, I could hear birds chirping from his end of the radio. Well, this was one hell of a report: my dad's crew set up a long-range radio transmitter, electrified most of the island, and somehow attracted all the missing birds, while the traveling band had basically done nothing but land the plane without being consumed in a giant fireball and rescue a janitor. Oh yeah, there aren't any fucking birds here.

My pathetic-ness was almost guaranteed by this point in my life, but I still disgustedly signaled to end our nightly chat, "Well, I guess I'll call you tomorrow after I get with Easy."

"All right, I hope everything is okay with him." He fell back into his radio protocol, "Gray Fox, over and out."

I had to fight the urge to say, "Of course he's okay. He's probably running the damn PRISON!"

6

Stay Puft

SALLY DICK HATED her job. She might have only been on this island for a little over a week, but she despised waking up in a poorly lit hotel room and walking to this stupid doctor's office. She was a social worker, not a nurse, dammit! She should be driving around arresting these yokels for not sending their children to public school as the benevolent government required, not doling out hand sanitizer to a bunch of illiterate rednecks. The scavengers had found a pair of scrubs she could squeeze into and when the local warlord–or whatever the hell he was–started asking for "people with basic medical knowledge," she was willing to do anything that wasn't dangerous. Now though, she could see that all of these people were beneath her. She planned to jump in the next car leaving town. These people had gold coins, a Postal Service, a library; this building had become a small hospital, and there was even a rudimentary justice system. None of it was public. It made Sally sick to think she was being controlled by a bunch of fucking Libertarians.

The day was wrapping up and she was relieved that the only thing she had left to do was take some papers to Dr. George, then she could walk back to her sad little "apartment." The one good thing about the apocalypse was the exercise–she was slimming down to her high school graduation weight.

She made her way down the darkening hall and paused. Through the door she heard, "There's something strange…in my neighborhood…who ya gonna call?"

This was obviously Dr. George's thick accent, and a muffled reply came through a walkie-talkie with just as much of an Indian accent. "There's something weird….and it don't look good…you've reached the Ghostbusters."

This was odd. Was the Doc losing his mind and quoting 80s theme songs on the radio? He came back quickly, "This is Phantom Foxtrot-Niner-Niner. Is the team ready?"

The radio buzzed. "Roger. All HITs standing by and awaiting orders."

Zombies On A Plane

Dr. George was amazed–every member of his unit was still alive and none had gone AWOL. He would continue to force himself to think about anything but his own country. He didn't want to speculate on India's immediate reaction to the plague, knowing that once he learned the truth, he would either be extremely disappointed or unbelievably happy. The special forces cardiologist tried to put all guesses out of his mind. He had seen movies detailing all kinds of apocalyptic scenarios. A good many of these fictional plagues started in Asia; the real world-ending virus had started on the other side of the planet from India, and he was hoping his nation had survived. He was nearly giddy at the prospect of seeing his friends and fellow countrymen; they would surely be able to enlighten him on the state of affairs on the subcontinent. Mayor Collins was going to jump for joy when he found out the doctor had been the undercover leader of an Indian special forces group, a unit of NSG Phantoms. Randy would be even more surprised that they were not going to seize power and simply wanted to use his island as a home base. Dr. George smiled; he noticed his hand shaking when he pressed the button to relay his coordinates. He stopped when he thought he heard something and listened for any eavesdroppers.

That was code! Sally thought, excitedly. He had to be using code words and was communicating with his terrorist buddies. She dropped her papers to the floor and started walking out. Sally wasn't stupid; the doctor was calling his friends to come take over America! She wasn't going to let ISIS take over her country! She might hate the leftists in power now, but she'd be damned before she let a bunch of foreigners take over. She planned to go tell the mayor about this sniveling commie planning a terrorist coup and make sure he did something about It. Well, she planned on doing just that. In the morning, right after she got some sleep.

And she did just that. Standing in front of Randy was a very serious social worker / nurse with quite a story. He found this girl and her claims a little ridiculous and tried to reassure her. "Sally, I have known Dr. George's family personally for several years. I'm pretty sure he's not an Al Qaeda; I don't think he's even a Muslim."

Nearly sobbing, she countered, "I heard him talking to his Jihadi buddies! They want to kill all the men and make the women sex slaves!"

Zombies On A Plane

Sally was adamant. There was no convincing her otherwise, so Randy conceded. "Okay. What if we go talk to him and find out what is going on?"

She furrowed her brow. "But shouldn't we at least take a bodyguard along?"

Randy chuckled and patted the grip of the pistol open-holstered on his hip. "I wouldn't leave home without one."

He grinned sadly to himself. Technically, he had not been "home" in close to a month. As thoughts of his destroyed home flashed across his mind, he locked the door to his office and radioed Debbie to inform her that he was going to see the doctor.

She replied a bit panicked, "Are you okay? Do you need me to drive? I'm just right across Gunter Avenue and can meet you at the truck."

He should have known his wife of over thirty years would hear this as "I'm bleeding out and in need intensive care." He finally got a word in. "No, dear, I'm good. I just need to have a chat with him about something."

He realized with a start that maybe this *was* home. His wife seemed fairly acclimated to their new digs and he was actually glad he was here, in the center of all the civic activity. Sure, the mayor might be living in a partially lit courthouse office taking at least bi-weekly trips to the *Viva Ancora* for a hot shower, but he was helping people settle in. These newcomers would not have survived without the functioning island he had partly been instrumental in reestablishing. Randy considered himself lucky that one of his sons had been on the island and was currently in Birmingham looking for his other son; most families had been separated–maybe permanently.

Sally got into the passenger seat of the Humvee and Randy drove away from his new HOME.

7

Phantasm

DR. GEORGE HAD just finished setting a child's broken arm when the mayor knocked briefly then walked right into the examination room. The doctor had always liked the no-nonsense Randy, how the man always went to the source without pussyfooting around. Well, he had been happy with the approach until now; he could have been in the middle of a gynecological exam on one of the soon-to-be-mothers of the coming baby boom!

Even so, he was glad the mayor was here. He had been planning to go to the courthouse during lunch, but now he could just walk the mayor across the hall to introduce him to the other Phantoms. The team had HALOED in early this morning and their entrance had excited him well beyond just seeing friends he'd thought lost. If the Indian Air Force had jets and pilots to spare for an airdrop, then his country had obviously survived armageddon in relatively good shape. He was just waiting for the opportunity to ask his fellows for details about their home.

"What's up, Doc?" Randy asked as he strode into the room and leaned on the bed.

The doctor could barely contain his smile. "Mayor Collins! Just the man I wanted to see. I need to talk to you about something…" he trailed as he noticed Sally walk in behind the mayor, her arms crossed in front of her in a very accusatory manner. He just realized that she had not been at the office all morning.

"Yeah, I think we do."

The mayor continued when the doctor found nothing to say. "I heard you got some friends that want to get to know us."

Dr. George smiled at the perceptiveness of the mayor; perhaps he had seen the team drop or was just a good guesser. "Yes, yes! They do! There will be one less worry with an armed detachment of–"

The Mayor had been hesitant to believe Sally up until this point. But the more he talked with The Medicine Man the more he started to doubt the Cardiologist's trustworthiness. Maybe he really was not the Indian he said he was. "Sally here told me all about your radio conversation with your buddies from the other side of the world. When are they planning on getting here?"

Zombies On A Plane

"They are actually right across the hall. I'm thrilled to introduce you to the HITs and perhaps we can work out an even more permanent solution."

The doctor was about to stand when Randy leveled his pistol, "Listen you damn camel jockey, we're not going to have your final solution here! This is a free city and I'm not going to let you make my wife a sex slave!"

That dumb girl might have just saved them! The doctor, a man Randy thought he knew, had called his terrorist comrades to take over the island! He wasn't sure how they got here so fast, but the mayor was going to do what he could to stop them.

There had obviously been some sort of misunderstanding, Philip George decided, hands up in the surrender pose. Sally fussing around in the office must've been what he heard last night; she had eavesdropped on him and heard only part of his conversation. He had been so ecstatic to hear from another Indian that he had ignored the noise and now things have become so misconstrued that someone might get shot.

"Who do you think I am?" the doctor asked, slightly offended; he had never ridden a camel.

"I don't really care who you are, Mo *ham* med," he said the name almost as an insult, "I can't believe I trusted you. I know the Koran says something about lying to your enemy being okay, but *damn*."

What was the mayor talking about, "Koran?" Neither the doctor nor any of the team was Muslim. Maybe something got lost in translation.

The doctor stammered, "I think you may be confused, Randy."

"You're the one that's confused if you think we are going to bend over for your Sharia!"

The doctor needed to solve this before the mayor filled him with bullets or the HITs across the hall came to defend the doctor with automatic weapons. He would prefer neither happen; Mayor Collins just misunderstood.

The Medicine Man could see things going south in his mind. If the mayor pulled the trigger, the other four HITs would rush through the door, obliterating Randy and Sally both. Even if the cardiologist survived the initial shot, the unit would empty their magazines into a man whose only thought was to defend his community. Hundreds of leaking bullet holes would cover the mayor's body, his single pistol providing absolutely no protection to him.

Zombies On A Plane

If he was not dead before he hit the floor, he would slip in the growing pool of his own bodily fluids, sinking down to perish in a gory mess.

"Please Randy." Still holding his hands in surrender, the doctor attempted to gesture to put the gun down. "I'm not here to hurt you or anyone else, and neither is my team. What must I say to convince you? I am your friend."

The mayor's grip eased on his pistol, but he was not willing to be fooled by Ali Baba. "Where are you from?"

The Medicine Man exhaled, deciding to come clean about everything, "I am from Kerela, which is a predominately Christian region of India. I am the unit commander and my team members are: Mahatma, Sanjay, Rajesh, and Kumar. They are Phantoms; a commando unit in the Indian NSG, and including myself, there are five of us. NSG Phantoms are called 'HITs.'"

The doctor could see a dubious smirk on the mayor's face and continued, "We are only here to discover more about the origins of the plague; we do not wish to have any part in governing or policing the area."

"So are you a doctor?"

"Yes. I began my training as a commando; a field medic. After service I finished medical school and am now a cardiologist. From the little we know of the virus, it appears to settle in or around the cardiovascular muscle, so I was sent here to study that aspect of the evolution of the epidemic."

As the doctor explained further, the mayor began lowering his pistol until it was pointing at the floor. Randy was mulling over the information as it came and finally asked, "But you were in Alabama before the virus hit us. Did you know about it?"

"Not with certainty. Governments around the world were working together to uncover and stop a terrorist plot to unleash this pandemic. Mobile was one of the open doors they planned to use to get into the country. I was sent here as at first as a precautionary measure."

Mayor Collins was wide-eyed at the revelation that the government might have known that millions of Americans would die; he tried to remain calm by avoiding that discussion for now. Instead he asked, "What about your wife and kids?"

"That was a lie, but I had to keep my cover and I'm sorry about that. No wife, no kids.

Zombies On A Plane

I escaped the hospital with my life and your neighborhood was luckily where I found myself. I used the story of a family to gain your trust.

"Hell it worked. You deserve an Emmy for that one!"

Philip George wasn't proud of his skills at deception; he had merely done what was necessary to protect his true identity.

"I'm not gonna shoot anybody. Bring Mustapha and Achmed and the rest of them in here so I can meet them," Randy smirked. The doctor frowned at the jab before realizing it was in jest and returned the grin.

The doctor let out a seven toned whistle that the mayor vaguely recognized. Four obviously Indian men entered the room with submachine guns over their armored shoulders. "Mayor Collins, this is Mahatma, Rajesh, Sanjay, and Kumar." Each man signaled his presence at the doctor's introduction. "These are my Phantom IIITs; we are at your disposal."

Mayor Collins was surprised and honored that this team of highly specialized soldiers would offer to be under his command. He was taken aback at the insane physical fitness of these special forces soldiers.

The mayor wasn't a racist; Dr. George had different features from these men, but they all looked blood-related to each other, almost as clones from a movie he had once seen about assassins. It was disconcerting and added to their intimidating appearance.

The mayor introduced himself and shook the hand of each man before turning to face Sally, who stood staring, open-mouthed at the armed troops before her. "Everything is settled now. If you don't mind," he gestured to the door, "we need to discuss some things."

So, Dr. Osama bin Laden had tricked the idiot mayor into believing they were friendly, Sally thought. She was going to laugh when Chris Matthews started making jokes about these morons getting slaughtered. She walked out of the room and decided she wouldn't be doing any nursing today or ever again. She was getting the hell out of this place as soon as POSSIBLE.

8

The Running Man

BRADLEY GAGE OPENED his gym when things on the island started settling down and it became safe for businesses to operate. He salvaged gym equipment from his house and various gyms throughout the city. He had even been working with Gene on the idea to set up treadmills that could charge the batteries for the building. Since opening, Bradley had been using the name The Running Man as a catchy title for his workout center; he just hoped others could not see the humor in a paraplegic managing a gym with that name. The Old Friend was definitely sure they would not catch the reference to a movie starring Arnold Schwarzenegger. Even though everyone seemed busy with surviving in this small safe zone, they managed to keep the workout room constantly crowded, studying martial arts under Master Gage. Mary was beyond happy with this set up; she loved all the visitors even though most of their bodies were strangely devoid of hair.

Yep, Bradley was pretty happy with the way things were going and hoped Mo would hurry up and bring Easy back.

None of these people knew enough to have discussions about fitness, holistic health, or nutrition. They were clueless when it came to carbohydrate versus protein intake, and don't even get him started on sodium or sugar.

It was difficult to look past the fact that he had no idea what had happened to his mother and father, but he was just thankful to not have to worry about the damned zombies all the time. The last time he'd had to watch a body being devoured by those ape-things was the day Walt became their sacrifice and met his maker. Bradley would agree he had been pretty sheltered. He wasn't going to deny that the zombies were out there; the former running back just had no problem with not currently being part of the active cast. He kind of needed a break.

The bodybuilder opened the front door so that he and his monkey could get some fresh air. He enjoyed his daily ritual of a protein shake while Mary, The Innocent, caught bugs. The Old Friend heard the mayor call from across the street before looking up. "Hey Bradley! You ever heard of a PHANTOM?"

9

Chief Engineer Gene Stanley's Log 2

THESE INDIAN SPECIAL Forces guys are pretty handy to have around. Randy made them the police force while The Admiral is away with Mo. They also do routine causeway patrols. They have their own gear and so declined to wear the RoboCop suits, storm trooper armor, or any of the other warrior gear I was willing to provide. If you ask me, it would have been a morale booster for the entire island to see our protectors as Spartans or Mandolorians.

Mayor Collins has filled me in on some of their back story. He explained that Dr. George has seen active combat; he could have been trained to be a killing machine, like the rest of his commando team. He is still working in the office while they walk around with automatic weapons and ooze intimidation.

The doctor believes he can develop a cure or vaccine with samples his team brought him; this science is clearly beyond my understanding.

Most think I am a technical genius that can do anything, and they are right to an extent, but things like biochemistry and physiology are just not my forte.

I must make a report. The birds have returned! I cannot speculate as to where they have been; I am guessing that they had initially migrated away because of the carnivorous peevies, or "blunatics," as I have come to call them, but in any case, they have now returned. Perhaps they are attracted to cities full of people.

I'm not sure why birds would be scared of the zombies; they can't fly, and they are far from silent when they climb trees. Our avian friends only began reappearing this morning or late last night, so I'm not sure if they are flocking to our peevie-free island and to the surrounding tiny, uninhabited islands, or are back to their normal environments everywhere. I will have to research this across other areas and record my findings.

Georgia and Hunter have officially moved in to Excelsior. Hunter is beyond ecstatic to be able to spend most of his free time on my Xbox and Georgia is enjoying all the other pleasures of the uncommon electricity.

Zombies On A Plane

She doesn't mind that I tell everyone: "THERE'S A GIRL LIVING WITH ME!" It feels great to be able to say that. Mayor Collins reported that Mo radioed last night and informed him that the search party would remain in Jefferson County until today. I can't wait to tell Mo THERE'S A GIRL LIVING WITH ME!"As a final note, a citizen of the City of Guntersville has gone missing. Sally Dick, a nurse that worked for Dr. George. She has vanished without a trace.

There have been no bodies found in the lake, no goodbye letter, nor desiccated body in her apartment. She simply disappeared. I speculate that this could possibly be the first murder on the island after the post-apocalyptic reconstruction–or it could just be that she got bored and wandered off sometime this morning. I will update the situation as I get NEWS.

Javan Bonds

10

Mo Journal Entry 5

"CRACKA, I AIN'T got no idea da hell you's talkin' bout."

"While you slept you kept saying 'Doris…Doris, oh Doris!'"

The Oracle and I bickered as he drifted the plane slowly to the shore. We would soon be making our way to the prison and hopefully, to my brother.

"That's my grandmother's name. You got something for old ladies?"

"Dat just a dignified name for a classy lady, fo sho."

I was actually intrigued. "Really? When did this happen? The only ladies I know with that name have blue hair. That name is just as modern sounding as Rose – Crow's secret given name."

I'm still a little pissed she never told me she had a name besides Crow, but the more I think about it, the more I realize I don't give a shit.

I am now picturing a love scene between Petunia and Rose. Oh Jesus. I need to stop thinking! All I can see is a huge bush of hair!

"Twas back in da day, yo," Smokes stated with a faraway look in his eye. I couldn't help myself.

"Yeah it would have to be. She's in her eighties!"

"Listen dick biscuit, I ain't inta dem mature women and I don't even like grilled cheese."

I had to stop and think about that. I threw up in my mouth a little bit as I tried to shake off that mental picture. He had won the argument and I was silent. Following that, I came to the realization that I had not thought about my grandparents since the peevies, and it sickened me. Parents, siblings, and any other immediate family member should obviously be at the top of anyone's priority list, and I was somewhat angry with myself for completely forgetting them. I had found and rescued my parents, the love of my life, and was fairly certain my brother would be alive.

Zombies On A Plane

Would they be next? I'm not asking if they are alive (even though that would be great), I'm just wondering if they will be the next family members I search for. I feel shitty for forgetting my pawpaw talking about cows, trucks, fences, or my mommaw's chicken casserole; I tried to put it out of my mind.

Our group began traveling up the curvy two-lane highway to where we had seen the prison. I had absolutely no clue what we would do when at the entrance, maybe we could just knock, ask nicely, and they would throw the door open. Hell, we could even politely take our shoes off before going inside. I've seen movies like this; even if we walked to the gate with our hands up, we'd still be thrown to the ground and violently molested as they searched us. That got me thinking. I looked over my shoulder to Hammer. "Should we leave our guns somewhere before we walk to the gate where there will probably be machine guns pointed at us?"

"Nah, I'm sure they'll take 'em, but I'd rather them be in a dry building than on the ground. If they are going to murder us for walking around outside the place, it's not really gonna matter if we are armed or not. Just keep your finger off the trigger." She looked to each of us as she finished.

I turned to see that our new comrade had Adjutant wrapped around his neck and a pistol in his waistband that I'm pretty sure he didn't have yesterday. I guess The Expert had decided he was trustworthy enough to carry some protection in the zombie land.

I'm writing this and you are reading it, so I obviously did not get cut in half by a mounted mini-gun, but I was incredulous. Here we were, walking up to a possibly hostile fortress, and had absolutely no idea whether we would be killed on sight.

This was like the first quest when The Oracle and I were only yards away from hordes of cannibalistic nudists all to collect some fucking condiments. We had absolutely no guarantee of the next day, yet trekked across a dead island to add some flavor to bland fish. Now, we were ignorantly rushing into hostile territory and never once questioned our sanity. If we weren't in a movie, I really don't think I would be alive.

By the way, when I use the word "walking," you can take that fucking literally. I don't know what the hell is wrong with myself or this group. We chose to hoof it for at least a mile like we were Bible characters. Smokes just needs nine more disciples following him.

Zombies On A Plane

It is beyond understanding. If I had a time machine right now, I would go back in time and knock the piss out of myself. Not a single member of the quartet even suggested commandeering a fucking rowboat to ease up the damn creek. The group was composed of me, an extremely lazy good for nothing; The Oracle, an extremely lazy, husky drug dealer who will undoubtedly be diagnosed diabetic in the near future; The Expert, a woman who probably already gets the senior discount on her coffee at Hardee's and is sporting the scars of recent injuries that would have been fatal to the average person. Add to this motley crew the newly discovered Loner, obviously born the same day as the chauffeur from Driving Miss Daisy. Not a single damn one of us had the foresight to say, "Hey, you know what would be a good idea? Fucking motorized transportation!"

The undead remained in the shadows of the woods; there was enough yardage between us and them to get a shot off if they decided to rush us. We were safe unless one of us started bleeding. We could catch glimpses of these blunatics fighting over pieces of torn woodland creatures, occasionally drawing blood by biting each other on the cheeks. One would rip a stringy piece of meat from whatever random animal the other was tearing into and then the one clutching the bloody feast would turn to snap at the thief.

Rivulets of peevie blood dripped down the chin of the protector of its food to become indiscernible from the other various fluids and bloodstains across the monster's face and chest.

It was creepy watching the beasts follow us down the two lane road from the precipice of the shadows. They were keeping their eyes on us, surely praying to their blue deity for a cloud to suddenly darken the sky. I witnessed one thing that I have never come across and I immediately wanted to wash my eyes with bleach: peevies fucking. I guess it was arousing to be within throwing distance of food; all the males could pitch a tent with the poles they were sporting. I guess prey just puts them in the mood to hump. A yellow-eyed nudist stood behind a female, skinny as a concentration camp victim, and just went at it doggie style! I'm not sure if Mr. Minuteman typically got in and got out so quick or if the speed mating was caused by the virus, but after just a few seconds he bucked with a shrill squeal. The moment he let loose, so did she. And I'm not talking about an earth shattering orgasm.

The female forcefully blew chunky bowel butter for an exceptional amount of time all over its assailant's abdomen. When the male blunatic dismounted, I was able to take in one of the most vomit inducing sights I can recall.

Zombies On A Plane

Its sagging testicles were coated in some type of running, sticky substance that had the consistency of maple syrup, framed by dripping shit trickling down its legs and all around its pubic area. Thinking about that reminds me of candy where the best part is on the inside– holy fuck, that was a disturbing thought! I don't think I'll ever be able to eat a Reese's Cup again. Now the question: "How many licks does it take to get to the center of a Tootsie Pop?" keeps running through my mind. God, I need a therapist. It was sickening to see what one would normally find in an adult film as a casual "wham, bam, thank you ma'am" in the woods and bathed in freezing water. What was more sickening was the fact that I had closely watched the animal baby-making dance and I continued to study the hairy, body fluids-soaked, private area of the male cannibal after it was over. I've seen some weird fetish porn, but if I ever decide to take the easy way out, I'm sure you will find this scene, which will forever be burned into my conscience, mentioned in the suicide note.

That brings another question to my mind. Are we going to have to worry about a second generation of peevies? Well, unless the virus makes the gestation period similar to canines or something, I think we'll be okay for at least eight more months.

I wonder if peevie 2.0 will come out just like a normal baby, or if mama zombie will spawn some type of sharp toothed werewolf. Shit, now I'm scaring myself.

At some point during our self-imposed march, Smokes hung his head. "White cops gonna beat da shit out us."

"Hell, we might get off easy; they could be black," I snickered.

"Mufucka, I been stopped for DWB," I had heard this before, but he clarified it at my cocked eyebrow, "Driving while black. 'Sides, you white; you a cop."

I nearly exploded with laughter. "Unless you are Ving Rhames, right?"

I was referring to the only argument I had ever witnessed in which he had been embarrassed and had clearly lost. He froze in place and narrowed his eyes at me as if he intended to make some type of ridiculous threat against my "cracka ass," but eventually he just grunted and continued walking like neither one of us had spoken.

We moved in relative silence until we approached a large sign alerting us we were coming upon the Joseph A. Davidson Alabama State Correctional Facility.

Zombies On A Plane

The four of us did as Hammer instructed and interlaced our fingers over the top of our heads as we crossed in front of the entrance.

"Fucking freeze! On your knees and turn around," came the bullhorn-enhanced command from somewhere above us.

I forced myself not to mention to the voice it would be somewhat difficult to turn around once we are already on our knees, simply doing a 180 and dropping to my knees in compliance. I really don't know why I'm an asshole; I can see it quite clearly. Even when I've literally got a gun to my head, I just feel compelled to be a smartass. I could see the Oracle out of the corner of my eye and noticed a twitch in his cheek, he was clearly thinking about the same thing. What sounded like a small gate was thrown open and at least two or three jackbooted guards could be heard stomping in our direction.

The Expert spoke softly through the corner of her mouth, "Just give them anything they want."

Really? What if they want to make me pregnant? I'm not sure if it was some sort of billy club or the butt of a rifle that connected with my temple, but my last conscious thoughts before my face impacted the pavement circled the question of: "Why the hell didn't we send just one person to the GATE?"

Javan Bonds

11

Mo Journal Entry 6

Prophecy from *The Book of Smokes*

Throughout the entire journey there will be several inevitable characters. One of these roles is The Dictator. One dictator will never meet the next, and whether the current dictator simply dies or disappears, there can only be one at a time. This character is a major antagonist, and while not necessarily connected to The Villain, is always seen as an enemy before long. This character may have good intentions, even plans for creating a better world, but will eventually realize they can only control others through tyranny and they happily accept that role.

"...Happens nearly every day. Just don't leave any cans of ale around him."

"How long does it usually take for him to wake up?"

Before Hammer could respond, I shot up to glare at her and raised a finger. "They hit me in the head with a blunt object!" I began, noticing now that I was still woozy and moving fast was probably not a good idea.

"It's not fainting when your brain bounces off your skull!"

I was sitting up from where they laid me on the floor. I looked to The Expert, there was a huge wad of tobacco sticking out of her cheek. I could not see a bloodied lip or a goose egg on her head anywhere. I turned to The Oracle who was nervously drumming his fingers on his knees, but was not injured. Finally, I turned to The Loner and saw no injury there, just that damn cat lying across his shoulders.

I was incredulous. "Why the hell didn't they hit y'all?"

"You are the only white male that is anywhere near healthy. They didn't want to carry him," she said pointing at Smokes. "And they thought he was an actor, pointing at Tychus." Then she poorly attempted to sound pitiful. "And I'm just a defenseless, weak little woman!"

I scoffed, weak my ass. That was almost laughable. At least I'm not the only one who thinks Tychus should be giving me true facts, and I can't fault anyone for not having a crane to move Smokes' lifeless body. I guess I'm somewhat flattered to be considered a reasonable facsimile of physically fit. Not that anyone could confuse my pasty form for anything but a white kid from the country.

"We ain't in a prison cell, so I guess that's a good sign," I said as I stood, leaning on the bench beside me.

"Dey ain't gotta put us in a cage to kill us, white bread."

I contemplated that and it made sense. I was hoping for some kind of reassurance from the Oracle, of course at this instance, he was not forthcoming. My first thought was that he did not know what was about to happen. I immediately realized that doubting his prophetical abilities was foolish. He simply wanted to leave me guessing.

We were in some type of waiting room. There were no bars or armed security guards to remind us that we were in a prison. No one spoke until Smokes looked at me, disgusted. "Damn son, you got sumpthin' in yo ass?"

Was the clenching and unclenching of my butt cheeks that obvious? I didn't feel that I was gritting my teeth. "Did they separate us?"

"Kinda, but they never had us more than across the room from one another," The Expert helpfully supplied.

I was about to ask if there had ever been a large obstacle between my unconscious body and her line of sight. The Oracle exploded, "Mufucka, ya pants was up da whole time!"

Being knocked out and butt raped is something I fear more than my brother fears spiders. I was still not sure. "Well, it's possible!

I've seen–" my imagination was reeled back in as the door violently swung open and two men with pistols at the ready marched in before pointing at Smokes, "Fat guy…you first!"

He looked somewhat offended but managed to keep his damn mouth shut for once and followed unquestioningly.

After nearly fifteen minutes, the guards returned without the Oracle and called for "Morgan Freeman!" Tychus followed with some hesitation, but went, regardless of his preference. Hammer and I were left to contemplate our deaths. Really? Cannibals? If so, Smokes would keep them busy for a while. Were they collecting peevies and feeding people to them? I was just praying they knocked me unconscious before they raped me.

I wasn't sure if she was trying to reassure me or calm herself down. "They are just sending us to talk to their boss one at a time, then separating us after just to keep the rest of us in the dark."

That could actually be what was happening, I was just positive it had something to do with forced anal entry.

The pair of guards returned without the janitor, "Okay, lady. You're up!"

"Just tell them the truth," she said over her shoulder as she stood to follow the uniformed men.

What the hell did I have to lie about? I came here looking for my brother and I saw no reason not to tell them that.

Besides, I was about to get foreign objects inserted into me; I would've told them about the map on the back of the U.S. Constitution if that would buy me a quicker bullet. I was not surprised that I was the last of our group to be taken; I get to think about how my friends are being tortured while I wait for the gimp. Maybe he preferred blacks and women; hopefully he would be exhausted and just shoot me.

Shit. The door swung open before I was ready. "Your turn, Buck-o!"

I was forced into a room with a pistol jammed into my kidney. I knew it was nothing compared to the pain that was to come during my molestation. I was seated in front of a nearly empty office desk. There were exotic game trophies mounted on all four walls of the room. I was appreciating the natural light in the office–this, like all the others I had entered in the past month–except the ones in the Guntersville Island courthouse–was completely without electrical power. There weren't any personal pictures on the walls and none on the desk.

I was attempting to focus on the animal heads and not think about what they did to my friends or what was about to happen to me. It was my personal, irrational fear and I kept coming back to it. Was he just going to bend me over this desk? Was there going to be a ball gag?

Zombies On A Plane

I knew I couldn't get away; the guards had stepped against the back wall with their hands on their holstered pistols.

I heard their walkie-talkies buzz and alert them that "Warden Slice is on the way." Slice? like Kimbo? I almost burst into tears. Here it was; I was about to get beat up and raped.

I remained facing away from the door as it opened. I started trying to hyperventilate myself as the heels clicked on the floor. Holy shit, I thought, the massive street fighter was wearing stilettos. I was trying not to scream as he walked around the desk.

I glanced up through squinted eyes and barely choked back another scream. Steven Tyler? I was immediately wondering why he would enjoy man butt when he could have any woman alive. I began hoping he would sing "Dream on" or "Back in the Saddle" while giving it to me; it might not be so bad. I opened my eyes fully and realized that this was neither a UFC champ nor the lead singer from Aerosmith. It was a tall, slender, light-skinned black woman in her mid-forties, actually fairly attractive.

Suddenly rape didn't sound so horrifying. I was just disappointed she probably wouldn't be willing to sing "Love In An Elevator" during our liaison. I confusedly asked, "So, you're not gonna rape me?"

"Excuse me?"

Shit, I don't think I could listen to this woman sing anyway. She shared the last name and the voice of Kimbo Slice.

I nearly laughed as I started imagining a video for "Dude Looks like a Lady" starring her–oh come on, I had just been thinking about Aerosmith.

I wisely kept my joke to myself as she sat behind the desk and began rifling through papers. "What is your name?"

I decided that this was either a personable rapist or that I was probably safe. "Mo–" I realized she was writing this down. "Collins."

"And where are you from?"

I was kinda relieved that she did not make any comments about *MadTV*. I started, "Well, I was born in Georgia and then we moved to–"

She waved her hand. "No, I mean where do you currently live?"

The warden's line of questioning continued for what seemed like hours until she finally dismissed me to another room. This time I was glad to be greeted. "What up dawg? She touch yo naughty places?"

I was glad to see that none of my comrades appeared to have been violated and sat down. Hammer tsk-tsked. "See, I told you they just wanted to get our stories separately."

Well shit. I guess she was right. I was a bit confused. "So why did they stick us in here and what happens now?"

The Expert reassured, "I reckon somebody will be in here shortly to let us know that our stories checked out–"

I shot a look over at Smokes as I interrupted him. "That is, if he didn't fuck it up."

He looked shocked and offended, "Mufucka, I pass wit flyin' cullas"

We discussed the questions we were asked until the warden walked in again. "It looks like your stories match up; I don't think it will be a problem if y'all want to stay here for a while as long as you pull your own weight…" she added as if she'd forgotten, "…oh, and you are looking for your brother? We do currently have an Ezekiel Collins living here. I will get you his information before you leave."

Holy shit, I would have kissed her had she not been so scary. "Wow! Thank you," was all I could muster.

We should have asked her about our weapons and what she meant by "pulling our own weight." I wonder if she can play the guitar? Dance? I'm not betting she can sing, but it would be pretty cool to at least watch her lip-synch.

Just as I felt that I had guessed the official role of the warden, I looked to The Oracle, who answered my unspoken question: "Dat da Dictata, WATSON."

12

Who You Gonna Call

THE NSG UNIT was able to bring very little information with them; Dr. George really knew nothing that he didn't know yesterday. The civilized world had been overcome so quickly, there had not even been time to dub it with any sort of official and proper name. "It" was simply known as "the infection" or "the virus." The Medicine Man wasn't going to label it anything. He wasn't willing to have the plague that destroyed the Western world called "George's Syndrome." It didn't really need any other name, "blue death," "the turning plague," and the hundreds of other nicknames the island residents had given to the affliction were simply playful and did not stick. Philip George could never bring himself to think of it as anything but "the infection." Not one of the recovered articles or medical journals the team had brought with them were worth a grain of salt to the cardiologist. USAMRID had at least had the time to do a few preliminary tests and studies on symptoms and reactions, but there had not been enough time for anyone to work on a vaccine.

To learn anything new, he supposed he would have to get a living infected and do his own research. With his Phantoms here, that became possible.

With the island's dozens of cattle, his HITs could use one as bait and easily procure one of the infected who the HITs agreed to casually call peevies. After some group planning with his Phantoms, he was hoping the mayor would not take much convincing.

A sample of an infected heart could eventually bring about an end to the sickness that had destroyed the world and possibly put homo sapiens back on the top of the food chain. The Medicine Man was not elated with the idea of sacrificing a sick, defenseless person who came to him, but he was willing to go beyond his Hippocratic Oath for the sake of saving the healthy population. Sometimes the needs of the many were worth the life of a few, even if they were completely innocent. If an infected could think, Dr. George reasoned he would likely freely give himself to save the entire human race; wouldn't THEY?

13

But Now I'm Found

Prophecy from *The Book of Smokes*

From time to time there will be one or more treacherous individuals who will separate from the protagonists and ally themselves with an enemy. Another common occurrence is for a person who has been bitten to hide the injury, eventually turning while in the safe zone. They will, of course, end up causing havoc unintentionally. The Betrayer(s) can ally formally with a group of human antagonists to cause mayhem among those that believe they are safe. This character will initially appear–and may actually be on the side of the survivors, but will become hostile whether consciously or sub consciously. There is a chance this may become a dual role played by one of the main protagonists.

EARL BUCKALEW WAS seriously considering just giving up. He was sick of this shit.

Since he'd left that stupid cunt at the pawnshop, he had been living on scattered scraps he found in the various houses that he stayed in temporarily.

The pickings had been fairly plentiful at the beginning, but having to stay one step ahead of this large group of bandits was tiring. They couldn't be anything other than marauders. He knew from watching movies that guys with guns and four-wheel-drives scavenging around after the apocalypse could not be trusted.

He made the decision not to enter Publix that day, thinking he'd just start walking towards his house, maybe cool down before turning back to the pawnshop. By the time he was thinking clearly, he had traveled miles and could tell by the sun that he needed to find a place to stay for the night. At first he'd barricaded himself into a windowless room in an abandoned house where he realized that he could enjoy this life, scavenging alone, indefinitely. He didn't need to go back to that evil redheaded bitch; he was happy with cans of beans or peas or whatever and not seeing another damn soul. That was until he heard that explosion from down the mountain. He'd prayed that stupid dike had blown herself up somehow, but in the following days these marauders started appearing, cleaning out houses, *his houses*.

Zombies On A Plane

Earl considered making some sort of contact, but thought better of it since he had nothing to defend himself with.

He had slowly been working his way through Albertville and was somewhere near one of the chicken plants and the National Guard Armory with no real destination in mind. The former truck driver would stay with 431 and go south until there were no zombies or people. He could see himself alone on a beach, drinking out of a coconut, naked as those damn monsters.

The Betrayer had found enough Spam and bottled water in the house he just left to last for days, if needed. Earl was glad his old job at Frito-Lay had been somewhat of an upper body workout every day, his pack was getting pretty heavy. It had been nearly a week since he had seen any raiders and was confident he must be beyond their territory. He was about to start whistling as his boots hit the road.

"Freeze motherfucker!" came the exclaimed order from a nervous looking soldier. The GI was standing with a rifle pointed at Earl from around the corner of a derelict car.

Earl was amazed he was able to talk the soldier out of riddling him with bullets. The Betrayer was overjoyed to have finally come across a soldier, not a stupid redneck marauder clinging to his guns and religion, but an actual government employee. Though no longer in complete control, it was a relief to see a vestige of the old world holding on to some power. It gave him hope that the US Government could make a comeback.

The soldier, a skinny kid named Private Baird filled Earl in as they walked to the Armory. "Our unit is made up of servicemen from nearly every branch. Our highest-ranking officer is Captain Bobbitt."

They entered the front doors of the darkened Armory and rounded the corner. They came to what appeared to be a classroom, natural light pouring in through the windows. Seated was a large man who gave off an aura of a military commander. He sat looking through a stack of papers on his desk.

Bobbitt, The Villain narrowed his eyes at the newcomer before Baird could introduce him. "Who the fuck is this?"

The private stood at attention. "Sir, this is Earl Buckalew, a survivor–"

Zombies On A Plane

"Was he bit or something? Why in the hell did you bring him to me?"

Before Baird could stammer out a response, Earl cut in. "You know, I'm right here." He opened his hands at his sides before adding, "And no, I'm not infected."

The Captain raised his eyebrows in confusion. Earl continued as he gestured to the young subordinate beside him. "My good buddy here was telling me about the people down on the island and what they did to some of your soldiers." The former truck driver saw that he had Bobbitt's attention. "And I hid out for awhile with the bitch that shot at you a few weeks ago."

Bobbitt's look of suspicion and anger built. Earl could sense it was probably an inopportune time to take a breath or move at all, but he wouldn't be judged without at least trying to explain himself.

Before the officer could burst into an angry tirade, Earl began detailing his story beginning with the day of the outbreak until now. The Betrayer told of his time in the pawnshop, the layout and treasure hoard of that evil redheaded witch's lair, the horrible way she had treated him, and his yearning for revenge.

"Hammer," the captain spoke the witch's nickname after Earl finished his story. He began to picture the horrible things he would do to this woman he so hated and planned to destroy. His current girlfriend, Sally Dick, a survivor that had also escaped those horrible bastards on the island, told him a little bit about some of the leaders on this supposed refuge. She had not been very close to this "Hammer," she had not even known Captain Sledge's nickname. Sally had said she was minding her own business, making her way to her house in Albertville, when she had luckily been detained by a patrolling squad of Bobbitt's soldiers.

Jonathan Bobbitt wasn't born yesterday. He knew exactly what this woman was doing and had seen her type before. As soon as she found the commander of this outfit, she basically threw her clothes off and tackled him. She had only been brought to him yesterday, but the captain had fucked more since that time than he could remember doing in a long time. She assumed that putting out would get her extra protection or privileges or something; Bobbitt didn't give a shit. As long as she kept giving it to him, she could continue to think pussy would buy her everything left in the world, and even if it didn't, he was going to make her think it did.

Zombies On A Plane

Sally marched into the dimly lit room, planted herself on the edge of the desk, and looked over both shoulders before asking her big, strong, Army Captain, "Who's your new friend, Jon?"

"His name is Earl. He knows a little bit about the people you used to live with."

Before Sally could respond, Earl added, "Well, I actually only know about one of them, that redheaded bitch. And, boy, would I love to teach her a lesson or two."

"You mean that lady with the eye patch? Saw her truck the first day I was down there and she was flying a Gadsden flag in the back. I'm surprised she didn't have a Nazi flag on the other side."

Sally giggled and Earl forced himself not to roll his eyes. This chick was a moron. He would be more than glad to have the US government in control and was even a solid Democrat. Only an idiot would compare "Don't Tread on Me" to the Holocaust.

Still, Earl was curious. "So how long were you down there?"

The secondary betrayer drummed her fingers on the desk. "Close to two weeks. They were a bunch of stupid libertarians with that 'right to bear arms' and Bill of Rights bullshit. I'm just glad I've got a big, strong, government man to protect me." She finished by theatrically collapsing into the arms of the captain.

She paused before shoving her hand down the front of his pants. She added, "Oh, and I think that Hammer woman disappeared on an airplane a few days ago with a couple of those pirates. I wouldn't shed a tear if that old bitch got eat," she chuckled quietly to herself.

The former Frito-Lay employee dropped his eyes to the floor to avoid giving away his look of utter incredulity. He would be happy to work with these military guys, but he wasn't sure how long he could tolerate this retard. Especially if she was going to keep making historical references after clearly flunking out of high school.

The captain broke away from the sloppy kisses of his willing concubine. "So, Mr. Buckalew, do you have any ideas about how to infiltrate the enemy's camp?"

The Betrayer scratched his chin as a light bulb suddenly flickered on over his head. "Yeah, I think I DO."

14

Mo Journal Entry 7

KIMBO FINALLY RETURNED with a map of the prison. She pointed out where my brother was staying, one of the guard barracks. I was expecting to find him in some sort of communal housing, not a private room.

What the fuck? This didn't appear to be some type of utilitarian manual listing areas in the prison. This looked like one of those colorful tourist maps full of designs and catchy quotes that you would get from an ice cream shop at a boardwalk! Do they really give family tours of a maximum-security prison? "Felons and Children under twelve get a discount?" I could imagine the family-oriented fun that could be experienced while walking through death row with your young daughter.

What was Easy doing in the guard barracks? Had he been given an official position with these people? Why wasn't he being housed in one of the jail cells like is typical in a movie? How many of the people here are former prisoners?

I probably need to think about and ask these questions when I have access to a human, my journal doesn't seem that knowledgeable. I had guessed that if my brother was housed there, then the barracks was probably some kind of executive suite or something.

After walking down the stairs, exiting the building, walking down the sidewalk, and entering the building that the warden had pointed out, we walked down a hallway entirely lined by opened doorways leading to empty rooms. At the very end of the concrete passage, a door was securely shut. Somehow I knew Easy was inside.

Before I continue, I must ask: where the hell was everybody? I expected the prison yard to be swarming with people, but I had only seen a few office workers, the two guards, the street fighting warden, and not another damn soul. Since The Oracle pointed out that she is The Dictator, perhaps they are all being shoved into giant ovens or being used in strange, basement experiments involving peevies. Would that not be scary as hell? I know you've seen *Human Centipede*. Yeah, let your imagination run with that and be disturbed, just like I was.

Zombies On A Plane

The door was thick, and no sound came through. I had a strange suspicion that my brother was inside because, well, where else would he be? I assumed the thickness of the door had something to do with the fact that we were at a prison.

Smokes went to knock on the door and I quickly pushed his hand down. "Mufucka, yo brotha not like black people at his doe?"

I chose not to respond; I've been down that road before. I knew exactly what I was going to do–Easy used to do it to me all the time. I planned to burst through the door like Kramer from *Seinfeld* and scare the crap out of him. I turned the knob and immediately swung the door open, throwing myself through it. In the instant it took me to enter the room in that fashion, so many things happened…most importantly I realized that next time it might be a good idea to not be a complete ass and politely knock before entering.

My bodybuilder brother was standing on the opposite side of the bed, facing me. He was completely naked. Sadly, but not surprisingly, I've seen my brother shirtless thousands more times than I have seen a topless female. Before anger or shock, embarrassment, or even surprise could register on his face, I saw a fierce strain around his eyes–one I'd only seen in bad porno films.

I would like to say he was only polishing the torpedo, but it's worse. I caught a glimpse of one of the most beautiful black women I have ever seen bent over the bed in front of him, her perfect, chocolate breasts squished up onto the mattress, her round bottom swaying enthusiastically….Don't judge me! No guy gives a shit who the dude is as long as he keeps his ass out of the camera! Just as I started thinking that maybe it hadn't been such a bad idea to explode through the door after all, this goddess let out a bloodcurdling scream, released herself abruptly from my lucky bastard brother and fled the room, trying, unsuccessfully, to cover her gorgeous jiggling flesh.

By this time, Easy was aware of my presence, but was unable to speak. The only thing he could do was make a single frustrated grunt before he finished himself off in a pathetically lonesome arc into thin air. For an impossibly long time we just looked at each other with mutual disgust.

Every man has been interrupted while trying to squeeze one out, and I'm no exception. My mom has come pretty close to catching me a few times, which she has kindly pretended never happened.

Once, though, I was caught in the act by a very desirable female friend in high school and I made a split second decision to ask her to join me. I meant it as a compliment, but she never spoke to me again, and refused to partner with me in lab.

I've had only one horribly regrettable interruption during self-abuse and it involved my grandmother.

I was in my early 20s, still living at home, relaxing on my bed on a rare afternoon off. My dad stuck his head in my room. "I'm going to town and your mawmaw is bringing chicken casserole for supper," he said as he left, locking the door behind him.

The sound of that lock clicking and the knowledge of finally being completely alone put me in the mood for a little one-on-one with the Chief of Staff. I shut my door and downloaded a "foreign film." It was only 2 o'clock–I figured I had plenty of time to complete my mission, but I was sorely mistaken.

I was wearing stereo headphones. Note: never wear headphones during a private act of violence or while hiking on train tracks.

About thirty minutes after my dad left, Mawmaw used her key to get in and pulled a *Seinfeld* on my bedroom door as I had just done to my brother. She came directly to my side, and kissed me on the cheek while my hands were wrapped around my lightsaber, and I was just about to hose down Obi Wan. I couldn't exit the video, nor could I prevent the final stroke, although I did swallow the battlecry.

For years I've been trying to convince myself that despite the fact she'd brought lunch over on her own, she was too old, blind, or innocent to have had a clue what was going on. However, I can barely eat chicken casserole now; it took me entirely too long to convince that woman she could leave the room and I would meet her in the dining room after I washed my hands.

"Mo? Come on man!"

"It seems you kinda beat me to that."

My completely shameless sibling had no compunction to put a pair of damned shorts on. He didn't even cover up, just left it hanging out there for God and…everybody.

He seemed upset, not glad to see me as I'd hoped.

At the moment I could completely understand, I would be kind of pissed too, if I were in his place. "Dude, what the hell are you doing here?"

"I have come to rescue you!" I exclaimed, offended he wasn't thankful I had just crashed his happy time.

He gestured to the now closed bathroom door, "We don't exactly need rescuing."

"Yeah, I am sorry about that." I wanted to add, "But you gotta admit that was damn funny." Ah, maybe he'll see the humor in it once he put some pants on.

I pointed to the bathroom and the ebony goddess beyond. "So I'm guessing you know her?"

"Well no shit, dumbass. That's my fiancée!"

I was a bit taken aback. "Why didn't you tell me you were engaged?"

He figuratively face palmed. "You do know that zombies have destroyed the world right? I couldn't exactly call you."

"I'm taking that to mean that the decision was recent," I said to my brother's total deadpan.

In case you haven't noticed, my brother is not the same type of sarcastic smartass I am; he does not subscribe to my type of humor. I'm sure he cracks jokes and laughs with his friends, witty anecdotes involving professional football players, supermodels getting tipsy, how much better he is at everything than us normal people, and so on. We are just on two different wavelengths.

"Do you remember this one's name?" I chuckled as I asked.

"Man, I told you we are engaged!"

The fact that my younger brother didn't seem to understand that my question was in jest made it that much funnier, to me, anyway. I nearly laughed before he answered, "Akambiya," he paused before I raised my eyebrows for a further explanation, "Akambiya or Aka Ngona," he finished as if that were explanation enough.

In my world, a complete conversation between two men can be had with few actual words spoken, and this conversation could easily have been verbally one-sided. Not to say that the speaker must control the direction of the dialogue, just that the questioner should be able to ask most of his queries through facial expressions, posture, and other non-spoken communication.

Zombies On A Plane

I'm not questioning my brother's masculinity or manhood (that would be next to impossible with him standing butt-ass naked in front of me), he just lives among a different type of people, people who speak rather than grunt.

He finally decided to lay it all out at my look of confusion. "Aka is African. She's from Zambia. She moved to Birmingham to study medicine and we've been together for close to a year. We've been engaged for a few weeks and I hated not being able to tell Mama and Daddy..."

He trailed off and pleadingly looked at me before I supplied, "Yeah dude, they made it. Hell, they are doing great, even with everything that's going on." I waved my hand to encompass the worldwide plague, crazy people trying to be warlords, blunatics, everything. "We came down here on a plane and can take you and your fiancée back with us."

"I ain't sure if–"

Easy was interrupted by Smokes walking into the room and immediately stumbling back out like he'd been shot. "Listen here you stupid crack–oh shit! Get back, get back, lady! Dey's naked white people in hur!"

The Expert questioned The Oracle, who replied, "Hellz naw! Dey's got 'tess-tackles!'"

Does it seem strange that I had carried on an entire conversation with my brother and had all but forgotten that his junk was displayed for the entire dead world? I, like most heterosexual men, do not question our sexuality and I am not offended by the nudity of another heterosexual male. We never spend any time at all rating, admiring, or criticizing anyone else in the room, but I guarantee you I would at least *notice* any other person completely and unashamedly naked in the same room and it would certainly affect the conversation. I've just seen Easy's perfectly bronzed body so often throughout my life, it was barely worth comment.

As Smokes disappeared into the hall, I decided to act before another person's eyes could be violated. "Put some damn pants on before Hammer comes in here."

He pulled a pair of gym shorts from the floor and slid them on. "Hammer?"

I smiled, thinking of the similar reaction from our father and the month I would need to catch my brother up on. "I've got a story to tell you."

Zombies On A Plane

Easy was angry. "They really burned the fucking house down?"

I nodded my head. I knew he was only mad about losing his trophies. The conversation progressed and I had already described most of the main protagonists and their physical traits.

"Bradley showed up? Awesome, no one here will arm wrestle with me. Is Mary still with him?"

I again nodded and was a bit perplexed. How the hell did my brother know that Bradley was in a wheelchair or had a monkey? He would probably tell me, "Football players are like a brotherhood of awesomeness."

"So this comic book guy really has Darth Vader's suit? Badass!"

My brother didn't get my geek genes, but everyone respects Darth Vader. I added, "And that janitor, Tychus? I think Gene has some power armor that he should wear."

"Um, okay." Easy had no clue what I was talking about, but agreed anyway.

There really wasn't any point in telling him about Starcraft; or anything else not immediately important. My companions had remained in the hall through our entire conversation; maybe they were just giving me time to catch up with my brother, or maybe Smokes was deathly afraid of seeing any more white penis.

I had described The Oracle's prophetic abilities in detail. Easy asked, "You think he knows what's going to happen?"

I shrugged my shoulders as if I wasn't a firm believer in his zombie gospel. "Ah, maybe. He's been pretty spot on so far; so who knows? I'm not sure how much detail comes to him, but he's got the plot points down for sure."

The door cracked open just enough for sound to come through, "You gays both naked now?"

I sighed before putting my hand over my eyes, "He's wearing pants now, y'all can come on in."

"You is dis retard's brotha?" The Oracle questioned to Easy's nod, and my friend smiled wickedly before he added, "Y'all sound like twins."

That was almost insulting. I have to admit that while our voices are similar, that's the only trait one could use to claim that we were related. Even if I ate steroids three meals a day like my brother does, I don't think people would start confusing the two of us. In my first journal Smokes said that I sounded like a young, hillbilly Tommy Lee Jones; I would compare my brother's voice to Matthew McConaughey's. It's actually feasible that the two actors are related. Dammit, I wish there was still *IMDb*!

As I said, we don't really share much in looks. Besides the fact that Easy is in the running for Mr. Universe and makes me look like an albino midget, he's bald. Not because–God forbid–he has anything close to a receding hairline. He just keeps his head smooth-shaven. For a guy that spent more money on hair treatment when he was in high school than I've earned in my entire life, I was surprised when he decided to go completely bald a few years ago. It was weird at first, but it suits him. There is no way I could pull that off.

I turned from The Oracle and faced my brother. I asked, "When do you think you'll be able to leave?

"Aka is still hiding in the bathroom, and I need to go talk to her first. But in any case, I'm not sure we can go with you."

I cocked my eyebrow. "Why not?" I noticed the Oracle over to my side wearing his "told you so, mufucka" grin. I could have smashed it off his face.

Aka had courageously emerged from the bathroom by this point, wrapped in a bathrobe that Easy had given her while trying to convince her to join the rest of us in the bedroom. She now sat on the end of the bed, close to my brother, glaring at me with venomous hatred, which I assumed was partially embarrassment. Seriously, if she'd had something sharp I would probably have moved to the other side of my large friend. She remained utterly speechless, and it was like the disturbing quiet right before the postal worker opens up on innocent bystanders. Other than that initial shriek, I had not heard her make a sound. She could have had a very thick accent, but it probably had more to do with the fact that I was a disgusting deviant who deliberately burst into the room while she and a close family member were involved in intercourse and didn't deserve, now, to hear her voice.

Zombies On A Plane

What can you say after something like that? "Sorry I walked in while you and my brother were doing the no pants dance. Nice boobies, by the way." Maybe I should simply have given her a thumbs UP?

Javan Bonds

15

Mo Journal Entry 8

"Y᎒ᴏᴜ ᴀʀᴇ sʜɪᴛᴛɪɴɢ me!" it was unbelievable what my brother was telling me. Scratch that, it *would be* unbelievable if my life was not a fucking horror movie. I had hoped to star in a unique, exciting-in-a- mediocre sort of way version, instead of your run-of-the-mill zombie flick, but I guess us mortals gotta take whatever The Screenwriter dishes out.

Easy shrugged his shoulders to tell me it was true. Warden Slice was the typical dictator. She believed she could create a stronger society from the remnants of the old by using citizens as prisoners to farm and work for the community. Maybe her idol was George Orwell.

Holy shit, I had to say it. I asked flatly, "Some animals are more equal than others?'"

My brother nodded sadly. He answered "Yeah, pretty close."

"So, what happened to all the prisoners?"

He sighed as he began. "We were told some of them escaped when this first started, long before we got here," he turned green as he continued, "and they fucking executed anyone who got violent. Then they got rid of any of the others that weren't willing to work, silent protestors, then they took out those folks that just weren't capable; said they were just taking up needed space as more people flowed in."

Someone, like Easy, who spent most of his life around me should have known that wouldn't be enough information. I wanted the whole story. "Well, that wasn't everyone, was it?"

He looked disgusted. "No, they–they're–shit, Mo. They're keeping a bunch chained up in one of the cellblocks during the day and secure them to the outer fence at night."

I was briefly confused until realization struck me. I began to ask before catching myself, "But why–fuck me! They get them infected on purpose?"

"Well, they always say it's an accident," he mumbled. "A pretty damn convenient accident if you ask me."

Zombies On A Plane

The Oracle spoke up and looked at me. "Cracka, why ain't you been hearin' me? I told you dat bitch was da bad guy, now we gotta fight our way outta dis shit, an I–"

I interrupted with a mischievous grin, "Wait, how can a 'bitch' be the 'bad guy?'"

The seer's nostrils flared and his eyes grew wide, "Mufucka dis serious man. I'ma..." he just trailed off, shaking his head.

I liked making those quick jabs but I wasn't about to start arguing with him sincerely. I had been listening; he never said that we should get out of Dodge! He wanted us to make a daring escape and possibly receive at least a casualty. He could have just told me what was going to fucking happen before we left Guntersville and I wouldn't have even gotten on the plane. Hell! That would mean we wouldn't have come across The Loner and I definitely wouldn't have found my brother, so I suppose we had to make this trip. There's either fate or there's not. There is, apparently, so that means we can't fuck it up no matter how hard we try. Smokes's mantra, "you's always at da place you is always post to be." flashed across my mind.

I tried to ignore the murderous glare aimed at me by Easy's fiancée. While he was still green from thinking about murdered people, I asked, "So where does that leave you and the rest of this population?" I explained my twisted thinking at his raised eyebrow, "I mean, how do they keep you in here? I doubt they threaten you with solitary confinement."

My brother tried to smile through his disgust. It became a scowl. "If you are not a good citizen, one who earns their quota and keeps to themselves, they just won't feed you. Or," he said, "they will make you go hunting with a bow and arrow." I furrowed my eyebrow. He continued before I could pester him. "But if you do something really bad, like fight or kill someone, they'll put you outside the fence at night with the others and use you as bait until you get bit."

I looked at my brother with both understanding and wide-eyed confusion. "That's it? No sex with peevies or zombie transplants?"

The unhealthiest person in the room broke in, "Da fuck wrong witchoo?"

I grew defensive, "It's a valid question!"

"Dat's fuckin' messed up, yo!"

Zombies On A Plane

"It's possible! People do some weird shit!"

"Fo sho. You just some lonely ass cracka thinkin' 'bout gettin' some head from da undead."

I was trying to decide if The Oracle had purposely made a rhyme. I fell back into the memory of the worst blowjob I've ever had. It creeped me out that Smokes could remind me of a sexual experience.

I already wrote that I met my longest relationship, Eternity, on the internet and that she was from Alaska. Before she moved to Alabama, she took a plane trip to visit me to decide if I was a serial killer that stalked fat, mentally challenged women online, or just some poor, lonely slob looking for female companionship. Any female. In that first week she discovered that I was so average that it was almost redundant. I discovered that she was a massive, and massively evil, bitch that I was, amazingly, able to live with. I guess it had to do with my expectations.

The day she arrived was just pitiful and it got worse from there. I was able to locate the airport in Huntsville, which I have never had a reason to visit before, and stood near the elevator waiting for her.

After a brief introduction, we got in my barely functional car and headed to the nearest Walmart, where, as we had previously discussed, she planned to give me a blowjob. If I had ever known a normal female in an intimate way before this, obviously I would have seen the red flags popping up everywhere. Anyway, not many guys turn this offer down, no matter the circumstances. First, I had never been to this particular Walmart and it took me over an hour to find it, though it turned out to be only around (the other) corner from the airport. Looking back, it would have saved me gas if we had just done it in the car, and would probably have been more legal. Alas, I can only plead retardation that began on the internet and didn't end until fourteen months later when her fat ass finally went back to Alaska.

Anyway, once we entered the store, we found that there was only one bathroom with a lockable door, the family / handicapped bathroom. I'm sure it appeared dodgy to the girl at the customer service desk to see two apparently healthy adults with no kids walk into the family restroom; I wouldn't know because I couldn't make eye contact with anyone. Once in this bathroom, I stood in front of and facing the toilet. Why? Because that's the only position I have ever taken in a public bathroom. She squeezed in between me and the commode, yes, it was tight, and pulled my pants down as she sank to her knees in front of me.

Zombies On A Plane

Before you get too excited here, let me tell you, this experience was the most disappointing sexual act I've ever had, and, well, that's a list it's hard to hit the bottom of. Without as much as a pat on the bottom, she just…started in. I could barely keep a decent hard-on; I mean, here we are at the Walmart toilet, and her technique just sucked–no pun intended. I actually looked down at my hand thinking it would be better if I helped her out a little. Naturally, you don't want to offend someone you hardly know when you are in this position. What if she went all Lorena Bobbitt on me with her teeth? Yeah, that thought helped me along. All I could do was pretend to enjoy it and hoped her badly timed chaffing of my sensitive areas would end soon. I tried to picture Emma Stone, but I was facing a sign that said "Do Not Flush Diapers," and had to close my eyes.

After entirely too long, I started getting a Charlie horse in my right leg. It gave out and I unfortunately managed to fall forward onto my assailant, I mean my new girlfriend's, head. When I collapsed onto her, I could see the back of her head bounce off of the toilet bowl like it was in slow motion. In that split-second I could only imagine the aftermath. As I followed her backwards landing spread eagle on the tile floor, on top of her with my pants-around-my-ankles, a mental image of a front page headline flashed through my mind:

"Local College Dropout Murders Internet Girlfriend During Sexual Assault." I sort of regret that she survived.

We laughed; who wouldn't? Looking back, it was kind of a high point in our relationship. She tried to get things going again, and, even though I'm not what you'd call a "Minuteman," after about twenty more agonizingly unenjoyable minutes I just tapped out. She looked up and asked what was wrong and I didn't know where to begin so I said "I'm just...tired."

This situation should have clued me in that I was teetering on the verge of the worst mistake of my life. I was impressed, if not proud of her for willing to spend an hour on her knees in that filthy bathroom, the way you're proud and impressed with a buddy that can eat two hundred wieners in ten minutes. But I was one sorry bastard. I'd never had less fun with a woman in front of me for any reason; I'd just wasted an hour, and I was embarrassed to walk back past customer service. If it weren't for the certainty of being mutilated then dying a slow painful death, I believe a zombie would have provided me a better time. The relationship went downhill hard from there, and I thank God every day I never have to see her evil, pudgy face again.

Zombies On A Plane

I shook myself from that nightmare while thinking over what Easy had told me so far. Did anyone else notice that The Oracle can carry on dialogue in front of any woman other than Crow? I thought that maybe because Hammer was more of a man than most of us could ever hope to be, he could say anything in front of her. But Aka could be Ms. Universe and he seemed to have no problems blasting "mufucka" out while mere feet away from her, or my mother, for that matter.

Anyway, I looked at my brother seriously. "Wait. You said something about a quota. Why the hell are you in here and not picking co–" before I could finish questioning, Smokes grunted loudly and I turned to stare at him. I completed my question, "Corn? Did you think I was about to say 'cotton?'"

"Hells yeah Grand Wizard, youse prolly 'bout to send me out there too."

Jesus, I slapped my forehead and was about to respond before my brother interrupted the argument with his smugness. "Yesterday I more than doubled my quota so they gave both of us the day off."

I guess even a communist dictatorship needs to prove that there are benefits to working hard. Of course, my perfect sibling is the example they would use.

A beacon of everything great, I was again reminded of why he's the FAVORITE.

16

Limbo

SARAH OGLE HAD just finished her midday shift waitressing TEOTWAWKI (The End Of The World As We Know It) Grill. She was heading into the courthouse to the offices that had become a temporary apartment for her and her adoptive parents, Randy and Debbie Collins. She had not realized how much Mo's absence would really affect her. Though he had only been gone for two days, she really missed him. They had not always kept in close contact in recent years. Maybe because he was a friend from before the apocalypse, or maybe because they had been spending more time together since he had saved her and his parents, or perhaps it had something to do with the fact that he truly cared for her–whatever the reason, she just wished he was here now.

Sarah had been through several romantic relationships in her life, but none of them had been much more than flings. Since she had found herself with the Collins family just over a month ago, her life had been moving so unimaginably fast that she had not had the time to even think about relationships, other than her faux-engagement to Walt, of course. After his suicide mission, which took out most of The Villain, she became free of all romantic ties for the first time in recent memory. The image of her best friend, Mo-Mo flashed across her mind, and she realized that he was the romantic tie she wanted. Though she had never let him know that she knew, it was painfully obvious that he was madly in love with her and had been for most of their friendship. She could see now that maybe she had felt the same way for just as long, only the timing just hadn't been right.

The summer they'd first become friends, they were inseparable. At one point she said to him, "Mo-Mo, sometimes it's like you're my boyfriend and I'm your girlfriend." She could see panic in his eyes briefly, before he laughed and brushed the statement off. She probably would not have remembered that single instance before the end of the world, but now that scene was vivid in her mind. She started contemplating how things would be different between them now if he had only given some kind of answer.

Zombies On A Plane

The Love Interest's inner thoughts were scattered as a man exited the courthouse just as she approached the door. He was a stocky, muscular guy with thin blonde hair and he wore a sinister-looking smile on his face. Not a "I just murdered somebody and got away with it" smile, more of a "I'm about to do something really bad and nobody knows it" grin. She had seen this mischievous look plenty of times throughout her life. She would have to ask Randy who that stranger was.

She moved down the hallway in a jog, feeling she had to hurry; Sarah had never seen this man before, but the look on his face told her that he was about to be involved in something horrible in the place she had quickly taken to as home. It was more than the slight smile of a drunk about to roll a friend's yard, it was the knowing smirk of a pickpocket entering a liquor store with a wallet full of a stranger's cash. With each double step, she grew more convinced that the guy she'd passed had the intent of hurting her by hurting the people she loved, ruining her small slice of paradise. She knew it wasn't really paradise, but it was close enough for her.. There were always monsters at the gates, but she was safe inside. She thought, *It's something like limbo; it might not be forever, but it doesn't matter.*

She entered the office of Mayor Collins. There were a thousand questions on her mind, but she was only able to start with one.

"Who was that MAN?'

17

Fraud

D_{AMN}, _{EARL} _{THOUGHT}, this is a pretty nice set up. They've got police, healthcare, gold, and they are even keeping their people well fed. The only things they are missing are running water and electricity. It just made sense that an island could be made completely safe twenty-four hours a day. He knew Bobbitt was going to use this enclave as his own after he killed the leadership. He decided that even if the military moved on after taking this sanctuary, he would stay here without the damn government.

Well fed is right; that fine piece of ass that just went by looked pretty healthy. Since everything started going downhill, Earl had noticed that the attractiveness of women had been going with it. He had no problem with chicks not being insanely fat, but he was never a fan of supermodels with eating disorders.

Hammer seemed to be reasonably fit for her age, even though she was a fucking dike. He could just imagine giving it to that stupid bitch while she bled out.

Every woman he had seen in the past month had a malnourished, tired look about them, like they were about to drop dead from exhaustion. Well, every one of them until that fucking Sally cunt, but she had come from this island where they apparently keep their bitches healthy.

From his conversation with that old guy–Collins or whatever the hell is name was, they were going to let him stay in a hotel room "until you can find a job." What the fuck was wrong with these people? They just automatically trusted anyone that asked for a place to stay? He was about to show them that not every swinging dick that came in promising goodwill and hard work was inherently moral. This act of fraud was easy and it was working out even better than The Betrayer had planned.

Sally told him Hammer had left the island recently, so nobody would know him. He was able to give the mayor his actual name; he was proud that his act of fraud had gone completely unnoticed. The Betrayer was certain he would get away cleanly.

He planned on breaking into Bottom Dollar and stealing everything he could before setting the place on fire.

Zombies On A Plane

As Earl crossed the pontoon bridge onto the island, he was escorted to a vehicle by guys in spacesuits with fucking swords on their backs! The former truck driver decided he would attempt to overpower one of these pussies when he started his mission, put the suit on, and bide his time before helping Bobbitt and his people across the causeway.

His first goal would be to figure out the best time to take down one of the guards. The Betrayer would let the National Guard Armory in on his plans over the radio TONIGHT.

Javan Bonds

18

Gluttony

BEAUSE ROBERT COE and Mortimer Lester had opted to house together from the beginning; they were bunked in a small house surrounded by other small houses that were gradually filling with the other survivors. Robert had been one of the many people to enter a relationship with what was commonly called his "island wife." While they could have been married by Bro. Williamson, most survivors were not dead set on a ceremony. They were ready to be part of the coming baby boom celebrations Mrs. Collins and her team had optimistically scheduled for eight to nine months out. All that was required was that the healthy citizens perform the task of fucking like rabbits to repopulate the earth.

Mortimer hated babies, the crying little bastards. Even though he had procrastinated, staying on the island after he planned to keep moving, the thought of an entire generation of infants on the island made the geriatric decide he would be leaving as soon as possible.

He was going to have to get out of here before these women started squirting out children. They had only been set up in this house yesterday; he had eight months to get moving.

Still, in preparation for his road trip, he had been hoarding food in his little room, taking charity from anyone that offered. The old man was saving up to get out of this damn little town.

Robert was denied entry; no one could know of his stash in case they wanted to be in on his great escape. He had scrounged for every one of those cans of beans, they were his! Mortimer would be damned if the stupid freeloader that had attached himself to the old man from day one thought he could tag along. He had another thing coming if he thought they were buddies. Robert had a truck in the driveway that he used for scavenging missions. The senior citizen hoped to steal it, drive over to the cattle company, attempt to convince that damned old preacher he had been ordered to take a cow for slaughter. He was a senior citizen, most people thought old folks and handicapped people were always trustworthy. He was confident that he could be convincing.

"Mortimer, why is there so much food in your closet?"

Shit! Dammit! Fuck! Now Robert will want to go with me, he thought "I was just holding onto it for a rainy day. What were you doing in there anyway?"

"Crystal found a cat and it ran to your room; I was looking for it." Robert added, "That food could be put to good use. I'm sure there are people that need to eat."

What the hell was wrong with this kid? Did he think this was some type of fucking hippie commune? This was his food. He earned it and Mortimer Lester didn't give his shit away to people that did not deserve it. Robert's stupid girlfriend had just made herself at home and thought she could go wherever she wanted in the house; well, she couldn't.

The older man responded, "Actually, I think I am going to do something with it. Just leave it alone and you'll find out." He didn't feel that it was gluttony; it was for a purpose other than simply hoarding it, after all. Even though Mortimer might kind of miss the idiot, the senior would load the truck with every scrap of food in this powerless little shack, appeal to that ignorant old preacher's stupid Christian goodness to get himself a cow, and then get the hell off this fucking island of MORONS.

Javan Bonds

Interlude 2

THE LONER AND my brother seemed extremely glad to see one another again, each assuming the other was lost when Easy and Aka left the dorm building with several other survivors. Both men pointedly skipped over talking about those students that left the dorm building with Easy back in May; they could only guess at their fates.

My brother told me of some of the untimely demises later, privately. Jason, Sam, Amber, and a few of his remaining classmates whom he had not been particularly close to had died stupidly on the trip to the prison. A couple of his best friends, Josh and Andy, had sacrificed themselves to save the rest of the group. Only he, his fiancée, and a few other insignificant characters had made it to their supposed sanctuary.

The two began telling us a particularly funny story involving some of my brother's extremely inebriated classmates, a freshly mopped hallway, and a fire alarm. Each man interjected comments into the entertaining commentary. Out of nowhere, Hammer jumped up as if she just took a cattle prod to the ass and politely excused herself to go potty.

Before the conversation could reignite, Smokes gave a cryptic prophecy. "She be back, foos."

I kind of expected her to leave the bathroom at some point. I could not understand why The Oracle felt the need to inform us of this. As she walked into the bathroom, was she expecting someone in the group to shout out, "Have a nice life?"And, sure enough, within moments she emerged from the restroom with a walkie-talkie in her hand. It took me longer than it should have to realize the significance. When we had been captured and interrogated all of our valuables had been confiscated: firearms, grenades, knives, and communication devices, we were left with nothing more than the armor on our backs. I looked at the radio questioningly and was about to ask how she smuggled it past our initial search. Suddenly, my eyes grew wide with understanding. Oh dear God, I hope it had been in a condom or a plastic baggie or something.

I wouldn't say it's impossible, the handset is not that bulky, but counting the antenna the thing was probably a foot-long. That could not have been hidden comfortably for the several hours she was stowing it away.

She held it out to me. "Your daddy gave me a buzz."

That would have been pretty funny if she had not been ready to hand over something that could be covered in her bodily fluids. I'm not really a germ-a-phobe, but I had to close my eyes and turn my head as I reached for it.

"Daddy?" I tried not to move my hand as I gingerly held the warm-to-the-touch device.

A sigh that told me I was a failure of a son for not sticking to radio etiquette came back. "Mo, Gray Fox. Any word on your brother? Over."

Easy stood up and crossed the room in record time. "Let me talk to him."

My dad's voice almost broke with the statement. "Easy."

I am normally unemotional and prefer to keep a polite, but cordial, distance between my male family members and myself. But I felt a pang of momentary jealousy when I heard the relief from the other side of the radio. I was glad my father didn't start bawling when my brother spoke, but I was betting he had to wipe his eyes. And that's perfectly okay.

There are only three instances in a man's life when it is acceptable for him to cry in the presence of others. Tears of joy is not really the same thing.

Reason 1: When the man is drunk. I'm not talking about when you are tipsy or just slightly intoxicated. If you get emotional after a few beers, someone will probably beat the shit out of you. You need to be a shot away from alcohol poisoning to earn the right to cry in public. If you have downed a half-gallon of Jim Beam in the past thirty minutes, no one is going to question your manhood over blubbering about your girlfriend who just left you because you are an alcoholic loser.

Reason 2: Death is before you. I don't mean losing your shit at your great grandmother's funeral; I mean painful death needs to be imminent. This really does not need explanation. If you are on your deathbed or if a family member is dying in front of you, you get a free pass to bawl like a baby.

Zombies On A Plane

Reason 3: When you are going away and possibly never returning. If you are being drafted to go fight in a foreign war, it's okay to shed a tear when telling your best friend you may never see him again.

It does not mean that you will lose the right to call yourself a man for crying, just don't start whimpering in front of me when you get fired from McDonald's. There's nothing wrong with crying; the dog I had for nearly fifteen years died the day before my twenty-first birthday, I sat in the backyard for hours screaming and crying. My defense, it was private.

Sure, I suppose my parents in the house, nearby neighbors, or people traveling by heard me wailing like a little girl, but I did not go to anyone with teary eyes and ask for comfort. Hank Hill is my philosophical role model; he would agree with me on this.

The fact that my father just discovered his perfect son was not lost was a pretty good excuse for him to get his eyes wet. I'm just a reject without a college degree that has been dubbed The Hero and could possibly be one of the saviors of the human race. I really didn't expect any more of an exclamation from him than he gave on our initial reunion: "Mo," followed by a handshake.

I was not surprised to hear my mother wail, "Ezekiel!" She almost tackled my dad as she charged into the room. After she affirmed it was truly Easy, she asked something typical of a mother, "Why haven't you called?"

Easy looked at me and I shrugged as if to ask, "What were you expecting?" He answered, "Well, I haven't really had a phone. Or service."

From anyone else, I would have seen this as an obvious joke, but my younger brother was deadpan as usual. She continued berating him with motherly questions and he answered to the best of his ability. I was surprised he did not inform my parents of his fiancée, but it really wouldn't make a difference right now anyway.

Daddy cut in, "So they're keeping you imprisoned in the prison?"

My dad could see the humor in the statement and I can imagine him making this statement, "Really, how?" The youngest Collins returned, "Pretty much; it's been this way since we got here."

"I guess that means your brother is stuck with you."

Zombies On A Plane

Well shit, I had not thought of that and apparently neither had Easy, who shrugged. We were both trapped by an insane tyrant that was surely a Democrat. We heard from across the room, "Fo now mufuckas."

If I had not seen him do this shit countless times, I probably would have resigned myself to never going home again. Strangely, my huge friend's creepy line bolstered my resolve. I didn't even know I had resolve.

"We're working on it, Daddy," I spoke as Easy held the radio.

"All right, let me know if you need anything on that." He was basically telling us to have fun during our ill-planned escape from a maximum security prison manned by insane murderers armed with machine guns and led by a vicious dictator with a God complex.

He continued, "Oh Mo, I wanted to tell you Dr. George turned out to be some kind of super Indian Navy SEAL. He brought his commando unit to the island." He somehow knew what I was thinking from over the radio and added, "And no, they're not taking over, they're just using the island as a base for their research mission."

My brother raised his eyebrows to ask a question and I narrowed mine, telling him I would explain later. "Well, at least he's one of the good guys," I told my dad.

"Of course he is, he's The Medicine Man," he confidently shot back, and I just knew The Oracle was fist-pumping. My father continued more casually, "And we still gotta find somebody to run the dam."

Aka spoke quietly to the two of us huddled around the radio. "I might be able to help with that."

I was a little stunned that the first words from Aka were not that her future brother-in-law was an evil deviant. I could detect no definite accent–come on, I'm not the only one that expects every African to sound like Idi Amin. She explained that she was part of the Chewa ethnic group from eastern Zambia and that her brother had worked in the local Kariba hydroelectric dam; she'd spent a lot of time observing the operation of the dam and had some clue of how to open and close one.

 News to me as well: black people divide themselves into even smaller ethnic groups. If I were to state that I was ethnically Irish and British I would just sound like a pasty white boy attempting to appear cultured, but it seemed reasonable coming from the ebony goddess that was my brother's woman.

Zombies On A Plane

Smokes looked like a fully clothed Buddha sporting an all-knowing grin; I guess this was another example of things that are "post to be." Now our only obstacle in getting back home was the insane prison warden, but I expect everything will turn out just like The Oracle has foreseen–actually, I will probably stay strong in my faith in The Oracle until something horrible happens and I almost die.

The one-eyed Captain casually mentioned to me, "Oh, that warden lady told me that we need to go see her in the morning to be assigned quarters and work orders." The silence was nearly deafening as I stared at her. She continued, "Don't worry, she said that we could just stay in the empty room next door tonight!"

What the fuck? When did The Dictator give these orders to The Expert and why is she just telling me now? It might not really make a difference, but I would like to have known the details of my slavery up front.

I guess it's a perk from our benefactors to be granted one night free from forced labor. I turned to my bodybuilder sibling. "So are we going to split rocks?"

"Why would you split–" he started to ask. He quickly clarified, "Well, no. You will probably be on farming detail like everybody else is to start out with."

He looked at Hammer. "They might make some of you guards or office staff in a week or so–"

I defiantly interrupted, "We ain't staying here that long." I was surprised he was willing to lay down for a despot. "And neither are you, dumbass."

His nostrils flared as I explained that we would discuss our escape plans in the morning. That's right, it was obvious that we were going to break out of a maximum-security prison in the next couple of days.

My dad rudely interrupted our conversation. He reminded us, "Hey, I'm still here!" He could then be heard speaking to someone in the room with him. He came back, "Mo, I've got someone here that wants to talk to you."

I cocked my head and was about to ask who it was. I was baffled that anyone would make a concerted effort to speak to me. A voice came over the radio, "I miss you Mo-Mo, when are you coming home?"

The Oracle chuckled silently. He incredulously mouthed "Mo-Mo?" I only scowled, telling him to make fun of me later.

Zombies On A Plane

I mumbled in reply, "I miss you too." I then added, "How are you?"

For my entire life, I've been nothing but a bumbling teenager when trying to converse with the opposite sex. Talking to The Love Interest, I could barely form a damn sentence. My goofiness is especially apparent over the phone or radio.

She came back, clearly in a hurry. "Everything's going great, I just wish you were here! Randy says he needs the radio back. I love you, Mo-Mo."

I don't know why, but I've always had a problem using that word around others. It's not that I don't love Sarah. It's just hard for me to say it even if it is meant in friendship. I just closed my eyes and stuttered, "I...love you, too. See you soon."

My father returned. "Well, we need to get off here. I'll get with you on your escape plans tomorrow night. Gray Fox, out."

Did anyone else notice how he drops out of his radio lingo whenever he feels like it, but because I don't have a call sign I'm a DISGRACE?

Javan Bonds

19

Mo Journal Entry 9

HAMMER ROUSED EACH of us as gently as my father would used to and just as damn early. The sun was barely up! I guess she was in a hurry to be enslaved.

"Where da food at lady?"

"We can go to the prison cafeteria." She paused as The Oracle's eyes grew wide. "After we go see Mo's brother."

He went apeshit. He screamed, "Aw fuck dat! Imma get me summin' in my belly now!"

The Loner, who was not much of a talker, ran his hand over his cat. He soothed, "If you show up alone, they'll start getting suspicious about the rest of us."

The future diabetic calmed at that. "Fine. But we gonna hurry da hell up or I's eatin 'y'all's skinny asses."

The threat was empty but physically possible. I gave him a little more hope, "I'm sure Easy has some protein bars in his room."

He shrugged in satisfaction and slowly got out of bed. We began filing out of the room. No showers, no brushing of teeth–we just took turns standing before the throne and were out the door.

"Do you know where they keep confiscated materials?"

"Why the hell would I know that? Just because I've been living here doesn't mean they gave me the key to the city!"

Really? They don't give prisoners guided tours of the prison, including a sneak peek at weak points of the fence? I simply sighed, "Do they have some sort of armory?"

"I guess. It'd be in the main building," my extremely helpful brother came back. He asked, "You had weapons or something?"

No retard, we would never carry those evil machines of death! Just because there are marauding paramilitary types and crazed blue cannibals in every shadow is no reason to go around armed. I know my brother isn't some kind of crazy liberal and wasn't asking because he just couldn't believe we would carry something so dangerous, he's just dense and sheltered.

The Expert cut in, "That reminds me! Hang on."

She stood and walked to the bathroom, returning not long after with a smile on her face and a handful of grenades. I started wondering if she had one of those hollow prosthetic limbs. Maybe the eyepatch is covering up a storage locker; there is no way in hell you can have five grenades shoved up your ass overnight and it simply slipped your mind. I wanted to ask her, "You mean you managed to smuggle grenades and a fucking walkie-talkie into the prison, but you couldn't stow away a damn pistol?" I thought better of it because I was afraid she would tell me where the grenades had been hidden, or worse, ask me to hide a couple for her.

"Frags!" she stated with a smile. "No shit," almost crossed my lips before I realized her response could have been, "Well, not much."

I stated the obvious. "I don't think we can bust out of prison with nothing but grenades."

Hammer rolled her eye at me. "I know that. I'll do some looking around and see if I can find where our guns are then use these things to get into wherever my precious little babies are locked up!"

My brother put his ripped arm over Aka's shoulders. "Wait...you expect us to help you escape from a maximum security prison? How do you know we can even shoot?"

I pointed at him accusingly. "Shut the hell up! I know you like guns as much as I do. Hell, I bet you money you've taken her to Hoover Tactical more than once." Hoover Tactical had the best firing range and gun store in central Alabama. I then swung my finger in the direction of The Loner. "And you were probably in..." I tried to estimate his age, "World War..."

He picked up the thread. "Actually, I was in the Guard during 'Nam. They taught us how to shoot."

I nodded happily, now knowing that Tychus was not personal friends with Henry Ford and that he had the skills we were looking for.

Easy looked away and mumbled, "Yeah, we went to Hoover Tactical a few times. Her favorite was the M16."

"Sounds like the start of a plan," began The Expert. "We'll case the main building and see what we can see after breakfast. We can fine tune the planning tonight."

The Oracle was already at the door, gesturing for us to line up and move. "Sko crackas, Imma get me some bacon and GRITS!"

Javan Bonds

20

Casing

THE SLEDGE WOMAN closed the door, following the other three newcomers out of the room. Warden Slice motioned for prisoners–citizen #263 and his bunkmate, to remain. She knew that Ezekiel Collins had a sibling among the four and hoped this would increase his productivity. "Good job in getting them here, 263. They will be safe and undoubtedly help grow our community."

If Mo has anything to say about it, we won't be a part of your community in a couple of days. Easy smiled and tried to sound sincere. "Anything to further the community."

This young man really cared about the proletariat and she wanted to show him the rewards of a true statesman. "You and 264 here don't have to rush to work today; you've earned a leisurely stroll. We have four new healthy sets of working hands, thanks to you."

He almost laughed as he thought: *I would say only three of those sets are healthy*, but instead he grinned as she patted his shoulder. "Thanks, Warden. I do what I can."

He and Aka were well away from the door when he felt they were out of hearing distance. He whispered, "*The Fried Green Tomatoes* lady told me to scope out the armory." He paused, wondering why Kathy Bates assumed that he would have the opportunity to do so. Perhaps she had been listening to fat Chris Tucker. "I don't think it'll be a big deal. You mind flirting with some of these stupid guards?"

Aka cornered some scrawny guard in the hallway and began seductively asking him to show her some "big guns." After only a few minutes, the rent-a-cop was fumbling out his keys and basically ran to unlock a door. They entered a room lined with more assault rifles than the African beauty had ever seen in one place. The sexually deprived prison employee was near passing out each time she softly moaned as she brushed her hand over several guns. She was unaware of just how seductive she was. This guy had balls bluer than a peevie; she was afraid he would spontaneously combust if she got close to him.

Zombies On A Plane

After only a few minutes inside the room, Aka slowly stood as she giggled, "Thanks for showing me all of this baby. Maybe we can come down here tomorrow and you can show me," she smiled even wider and let her eyes trail down, "some even bigger toys."

He nodded vigorously as he followed her out of the room. "You bet, sweetheart! I'll be waiting right here!"

The ebony goddess rounded the corner as she tried to shake off her disgust. She knew it was necessary, but hated flirting with the creepy little guard. This better have been worth it. She nearly screamed when she was pinned between two thick arms. "That was so hot." she didn't know her future husband was a peeping Tom, like his big brother. "See? That wasn't…hard. But I know what is!" She fought to control her laughter. He was just as weird as this Mo character and the nerdy little prison guard she had just tricked. Easy was glad to see that his fiancée was disgusted and asked, "Need a shower? I sure do!" She shrugged, figuring her job had earned her something, so Easy rushed her back to their ROOM.

Javan Bonds

21

Lust

Since discovering the small remnant of the US military residing at this National Guard Armory, Sally Dick kept her legs perpetually spread for Captain Jonathan Bobbitt. No, she wasn't some kind of nymphomaniac. She wasn't giving him whatever he wanted out of personal lust, wasn't remotely in love with him, nor did she throw herself on top of the man because he was a sexually irresistible monster. Sure, she enjoyed fucking, but she'd had better. Her reasons for keeping him overdosed on sex were much more rational. She was doing it for power. The secondary betrayer wasn't planning a coup, but the clever harpy wouldn't be distraught if he did somehow tragically die. She would happily make herself the queen of zombie land.

Sally was aware throughout history that women were the real rulers behind their powerful men. Strong kings were often advised by their wives, and even if much of her time was spent on her knees, she would tolerate it. It goes without saying that preferential treatment can lead to greater opportunities and that takes extra effort. Sally was willing to put forth all the effort it required.

Even if Bobbitt could see that Sally Dick was only acting as his concubine to become a protected principle, he would not be willing to give up his one pleasure out of some sense of honor or because of morals. It was almost impossible for men to put their job above pussy; Sally knew this and was willing to take advantage of their weakness.

The other soldiers already treated her like royalty. They gave Bobbitt a knowing glance and a smile whenever they saw him. Soon she would have enough influence to give commands and with the partnership of that redneck truck driver, Bobbitt's plans to infiltrate Guntersville should work out without a hitch.

Something came to her mind about taking the next step to command before the attack on the island. The secondary betrayer was gaining power so fast, she decided her dear Jonathan wouldn't be needed much longer. After all, her redneck was already in place. What was the phrase coined in Vietnam when a soldier threw a grenade at his commander?

FRAGGING.

22

Greed

HIS MEN TALKED about what they thought was happening or about something that someone had told them they had heard from someone who had been on the island. It had the feeling of *Zombieland*, people hearing things from people that probably didn't even exist. Bobbitt had nothing more than hearsay and rumors until his patchwork military company had come across Sally. Having been a resident of Guntersville just recently, she could actually give up to date reports on the island safe haven and the people that controlled the citizens.

He had to admit that he was a bit envious of this Mayor Collins in his island fortress. The soon to be ousted warlord ruled over seemingly dozens, perhaps hundreds of people. He had secured multiplying livestock, and he had a cache of gold! It made Bobbitt's mouth water just thinking about a steak; he had been eating nothing but MREs and scavenged cannedgoods for about a month.

The first thing The Villain would do after capturing the island would be to eat a cow's-worth of bloody meat. But the best part was the gold. He could imagine himself like a Saudi prince sitting on a golden throne. He had guns and he had the gold. People all thought he was part of the US government, and they would obey his commands, even if he had to slap some of them around. The Villain would gladly be violent to satisfy his greed. No matter what Sally said, he trusted that his men would be able to control the islanders.

No matter how much the damn libertarians thought they were free, all people obey a powerful government. He knew that Sally hated those people and thought they were Nazis for flying Confederate flags, but he had to admit that–at least from what she told him–they were making things work. She might be stupid when it came to politics and willfully dependent on big brother, but she wasn't stupid when it came to getting what she wanted. He knew that she was only fucking him to get protection, but he was okay with that; it was a fair price. Bobbitt had a woman that would do things he had not imagined were possible, a bunch of men with a bunch of guns that would follow him to hell, and he would soon have a bunch of mindless peons to control on top of a shitload of gold. He couldn't wait for that radio message from Earl.

Zombies On A Plane

There would probably be more than one casualty on his side, but the captain didn't care. All that mattered was getting what he wanted, what he DESERVED.

Javan Bonds

23

Anger

SHE WAS SITTING behind the desk at Excelsior Comics, waiting for another customer to purchase another book, deck of playing cards, T-shirt, or even an action figure. Since moving in with Gene, Georgia had accepted gold, goods, and even the occasional pre-1965 dimes in exchange for various luxuries.

She remembered calling Gene on the radio. She got his acceptance of the proposed payment, "pre-1965 dimes contain pure silver," he told her, "they will work as tender."

After she had agreed to live with him, he found her lying in wait in his bed and he nearly fainted. She found his astonishment that she would consider him "her boyfriend" to be adorable. Georgia could actually see herself being with this nerdy little man for a lifetime. He would do anything for her, but her first choice would have been Daniel.

She was still crazy for the man that was never coming back and it had to be someone's fault he was gone. She would never let Gene into that part of her heart, the secret corner that always imagined Daniel in the bed beside her. She wondered if all widows felt this way and if she could ever heal. Not only did she miss him, she was angry he was gone. She needed to blame someone for her loss; someone had to pay. That crazy old State Senator was already dead; she needed a living person to hate. The bereaved widow could hate that fat black guy. What was his name? "Toker?" Smoky?" "Smoker?" It came to her: "Smokes!" He didn't pull the trigger, but he's the one that cemented the awful truth in her mind and she despised him for it.

The man wearing the UNSC uniform was adamantly arguing with a member of the construction crew. He screamed, "I don't give a flying frack, it is feasible!" he came back at every complaint. "Put a solid slant over it as a roof and you can mount the 50 on a steel pole in the middle of the craft." Someone answered. He screamed, "I know this is just a bass boat but picture it as a PT boat! It will be very intimidating." Then, "I don't care what color you call it, you stupid piece of Bantha poodoo. Paint it Bird of Prey green!"

Finally he'd had enough. "Oh yeah? Well your mother has a smooth forehead!"

"But *who* are we trying to intimidate?" came back one of the workers.

Gene tried to calm himself; anger leads to the dark side. Only someone who had received nearly more wedgies than was physically possible could understand the importance of showing strength even if you think no one is watching. "It doesn't matter! The people living here need to believe that we can defend them. If they can see the photon torpedoes in the launch bay, it will just be one less thing for them to worry about."

The construction workers had been tasked with building this gunboat anyway, so this argument was pointless. Gene felt that he had finally convinced them that a strong defense is a good offense, whether the game was on the Xbox, PlayStation, tabletop, or an active war zone full of peevies.

Island dwellers only used motorized transportation in the city when transporting something large, so he didn't have to fight traffic on his moped, as he would have just a few months ago. The only other vehicles were bicycles and the occasional horse (or horse drawn carriage); he wondered why there were no other mopeds or even motorcycles in use.

Whether or not they ever found someone to operate the hydroelectric dam, he could see that in the near future that he would have to get the traffic lights working when automobiles soon re-appeared. His Jedi training told him that the Force would open up a path.

He was shaken from his reverie by a transmission over the radio built into his helmet. "Gene, where are you?" Georgia asked frantically. "I need you to meet me at the clinic!"

"What's wrong, Princess?" He made sure to end almost every sentence like that and she found it endearing.

"Hunter was playing on the playground over at the Methodist Church with some of the other kids. He fell and broke his arm! One of the parents called me on the radio and told me they were taking him to Dr. George's!"

"He'll be okay, Imzadi. Do you need me to come get you?"

"No, I got it. The mayor heard the radio transmission and he offered to give me a ride. Said he was going over there anyway."

"Okay, I'll see you in a few parsecs." He tacked on one of his customary lines, "And may the Force be with you."

"Tonight?" Randy asked.

"Yes, a full moon means greater visibility for The Phantoms, meaning more likely success for the mission." Dr. George was explaining to the mayor the details of the mission and what he could do to help. Randy knew of this NSG unit's overall goals and would do what he could, especially if there was even a remote possibility of the virus being cured. A vaccine would be worth every cow left in existence.

He pulled his walkie-talkie from his belt. "Well, hang on. I'll call the preacher and see if he can provide you some bait."

The cardiologist smiled, realizing the mayor had anticipated his next request. The noises of a bovine would be like a dinner bell for the carnivorous afflicted.

Randy clicked the radio on as he walked out of the room into the hallway. Dr. George turned to enter the examination room and check on young Hunter Daniels.

The Phantom doctor was surprised that the boy had made almost no sound while his arm was being set, even now remaining utterly quiet. Maybe the death of his father, Daniel, the genius behind the pontoon bridges and the draw bridge over the river, had changed the boy from a happy-go-lucky child into a silent recluse; it was too early to tell.. Since entering the clinic, the boy's stepmother had not stopped crying uncontrollably. Her apparent "boyfriend" had done nothing but unsuccessfully attempt to console her.

Throughout the setting and casting of the arm, The Medicine Man could make out only one of her many repeated phrases: "This is all Smokes's FAULT!"

24

Heresy

BROTHER WILLIAMSON HAD received a call on the radio from the mayor about an hour ago. Mayor Collins was looking for an "easy to handle calf" The Phantoms could use on a top-secret mission. He had been told not to expect the head of livestock returned; details would be explained upon the arrival of the soldiers. The Man of God understood. Even though the interim government of the island city had an official radio channel, it was not completely secure and sensitive information could be accessed by any of the residents. Soje Williamson was pretty sure Mayor Collins wasn't planning to make veal steaks. Whatever the "mission" was, he was willing to trust in the Lord to see everything through. He already had a young calf waiting in the catch pen, innocent of whatever fate might befall it. The Man of God was confident several soldiers would have no problem loading it into whatever vehicle they were driving.

"…They'll catch you up on it when they get there. Over and out." The radio transmission ended and Mortimer almost shouted with glee.

The old man turned Robert's truck across the highway to make his way to that old preacher's land. He drove by the Carr funeral home, now being used as temporary housing. Mortimer had to give these people some credit. The island wasn't crowded, but they were using all available space in the most prudent way.

Even though Robert and that stupid little bitch he kept around were too damned loud and annoying, it was better than hiding from dozens of those shit-eating bastards. He had enough nonperishables to last for weeks. A small beef cow that he could slaughter somewhere up the road would stretch his food supply for weeks more, possibly even longer if he could carry enough salt with him.

"I don't give a good goddamn preacher! Randy sent me instead!" Mortimer was just hoping that he had remembered the mayor's first name. He was hopeful this gullible religious fanatic would give him what he wanted.

Zombies On A Plane

This stupid old colored guy was really pissing him off. He didn't figure it would be hard at all to trick him into giving up one measly calf. This stubborn Bible thumper was going to waste so much time that those soldiers would be here before he could make his getaway.

Blasphemy? Heresy? Forgive them Father, for they know not what they do. "Well then," the good brother said, "I'll just give him a buzz to make sure thats what he wants to happen." Before he could radio in, a Humvee pulled up near him. "Guess I ain't gotta call no more." He pointed to the approaching Phantoms in their Jeep.

In the past couple of days, these four young Indian men had been taken in and showered with gratitude and respect by the islanders. They were being treated as saviors, though they had done nothing more than participate in routine patrols and keep the overall peace. The Man of God wanted to tell them that Guntersville simply appreciated their presence, that their stability and representation of support from the outside world made them feel hopeful and secure, and best of all, that they were not alone in the world. That little white kid with the cartoon picture books wanted them to wear suits of armor. People were really just glad to see a functioning, apparently moral military unit, regardless of its country of origin.

"So the mayor told you what we needed?" one of them asked in heavily accented English.

The pastor gestured to the baseball field. "Yep, I got your little fella in the pen."

The blood drained from Mortimer's face as one of the soldiers pointed at him. "Who's this?"

Soje decided that the Lord would judge this old guy in the end; in the meantime it was his Christian duty to give until it hurt. "Mr. Lester here was just pickin' up a cow." He gestured to an old and sickly looking heifer in the pen adjacent to theirs. "Don't mind him none."

Mortimer turned and began walking to his cow. He was still shaking after almost being busted. *Why didn't the preacher tell them I was lying and trying to steal their cow? Maybe it's something to do with that "What Would Jesus Do" shit.* Mortimer whispered to himself. Ah, who cares. They hadn't tackled him yet. The old man decided he was in the clear. Mortimer mumbled, "As long as Jesus gives me provisions, I don't care what else He does."

Zombies On A Plane

This old cow just looked beaten and tired. It would obviously be more demanding of care, but the old man knew beggars couldn't be choosers, and meat was MEAT.

Javan Bonds

25

Mo Journal Entry 10

THIS MORNING'S BREAKFAST was slop with a side of slightly darker slop. It tasted like and had the texture of something close to zombie shit. It was entirely worth eating the stuff to see the soul crushing confusion and then the burning hatred in the eyes of The Oracle. He nearly lost it when he found that his dessert was nothing more than a stale sugar cookie.

After our hearty breakfast of goop, Easy lead our group through the main building to get our work papers from the benefactors. To the surprise of absolutely no one, even Smokes was deemed fit for work. We were summarily sent to the fields, loud complaints about the "slave owning crackas" could be heard throughout our long march. I reminded The Oracle more than once that the warden was a black woman. Of course my reasoning went completely unheeded.

The enforcer watching over us with a shotgun was not directly threatening but he didn't seem friendly. It was pretty damn intimidating to be hawked over by a large man swinging a 12 gauge and wearing mirrored sunglasses. I should have been used to backbreaking manual labor. The only differences between this and digging the canal was that my dad didn't almost spit streams of tobacco juice on the workers or lord it over us with a Mossberg.

I barely finished the last entry during one of our rare and short breaks. I have no idea how I would have made it through the day without Smokes belting out perfect renditions of any requested song. I'm not shitting you, he pulled off "Hit Me with Your Best Shot." Yeah, I'll admit that I got sexually aroused when "Main Street" came around. Seger is one of the greatest.

I bring it up again, the warden is a black woman with white slaves. Of course, The Oracle and The Loner are also her slaves, it just seems like all of the white people picking corn were looked at differently by the guard. I don't think I interacted with one worker who was not in our private group of protagonists. Everyone else could probably be thrown into the Insignificant Character category.

Zombies On A Plane

I looked over to see the guy wearing the plastic badge pushing and screaming at one of the field hands. This brave but stupid worker was apparently not willing to be bossed around like a disposable field hand and had decided to push back. I wasn't sure why this altercation began. The picker might have been sleeping on the job or maybe the guard just didn't like the way he looked. I cringed when the slave made his stand, because I could immediately see what was going to happen. The guard bowed up and slammed the man in the chest with the butt of his shotgun. That would've probably broken several of my ribs, but the worker reached up a pleading hand to the enforcer. The prison guard let loose on the downed man and hammered his face and chest with the synthetic stock of his weapon. Bones could be heard snapping amidst the cries for help and the pleading for mercy. Two medics appeared from nowhere, forcefully manhandled the destroyed body onto a gurney, and carried the bloodied pile off screen.

Back to my thoughts before I was rudely interrupted by someone being murdered. Is this karma or irony? I don't want to call it, I might get arrested by the irony POLICE.

Javan Bonds

26

Mo Journal Entry 11

I COLLAPSED ONTO the couch in my brother's room. "I don't know about the rest of y'all, but I ain't doing that shit tomorrow!"

I noticed my brother grin at Aka mischievously. He agreed, "Yeah, it was a hell of a workout."

I glared at him. The bastard didn't even show up until it was almost quitting time. "So Hammer said you two were gonna find the armory?" I asked my brother as I glanced in the direction of The Expert.

She nodded as my brother began, "All the credit goes to Aka." He waved at his fiancée. "She teased that guard so much he needed a cigarette." He chuckled before adding, "We were thinking about it and we decided that it won't take a grenade to get in there."

He put up a hand at Hammer's start. "She can just get that same guard to unlock the door. I can come up behind him and knock him out cold once he opens it."

It's funny how quickly my brother went from a contented, warlord-pet pacifist to a bloodthirsty guerrilla. I was sure he knew several ways to knock a person unconscious with one finger. He seemed eager to wreak some violence on these mall cops. I was proud of him.

The captain shrugged. "Good thinking. That just gives us more time before an alarm."

I hated to be a killjoy. "Sounds great, but what about the towers? I'd rather not get mowed down by machine guns as we make a run for it."

The Expert thought about it. She offered, "We can set tripwires at the doors. We can also set them on fire as we go by."

I'm amazed this super soldier only lost one eye during her military service. Her idea of planning a mission was to hope that we would not get ripped in half by a mounted machine gun! I wanted to tell her that she was not Gene, she could not just quick load, and she only had one life, as far as I knew.

Zombies On A Plane

I was getting ready to call my dad to give him my final farewells. Professor Smokes spoke. "We need an alternative plan in case the schedule changes. We may run into unforeseen anomalies."

Fuck! Is this a joke, God? If he says creepy shit like that, you know something bad is going to happen. Well, maybe he just thinks Hammer's idea to handle the towers is just as stupid as I do.

A thought came to me. I looked at Aka who shook her head as the words left my mouth. I asked, "Did you notice any rocket launchers in the armory?"

Damn, I've been wanting to shoot a bazooka for a long time. I have absolutely no clue to what The Oracle was referring with his eerie "unforeseen anomalies" and shit. You can bet your ass he won't just fucking tell me. That'd make my life too easy; The Screenwriter forbid I ever get a break.

Easy brightened, "Some of my creams are flammable." The Expert smiled with agreement. She added, "And we can use that to make sticky bombs for the towers!"

I knew he was talking about the creams he puts on his face every morning. He probably spends more time in the bathroom than his fiancée!

I was glad that my brother was being helpful. I turned to The Oracle to gauge his reaction to our evolving plan, hoping to see some reaction that would guide us. Nope, not a damn sign. Nothing to tell me whether we were heading in the right direction or would face an unbelievably horrible death scene.

"We could take Kimbo out while y'all are raiding the armory, cause more confusion."

Smokes immediately fell back into his customary speech patterns. "Watchoo wanna kill all da colad folk fo, white bread?"

I uncharacteristically retorted to his accusation of racism. I poorly attempted to joke, "I've not even discussed with my brother my plan of getting rid of you. I'm waiting until you people leave to put on my Klan hood and light up a cross."

The room got deathly quiet and every person looked shocked or horrified. Even the white lesbian looked at me with disgust. Come on, it was a joke! Lighten up! I was about to begin my humiliating apology for the existence of white people and my crappy excuse for a sense of humor.

Zombies On A Plane

Hammer thankfully interrupted my Chris Matthews moment. She answered my earlier question, "Well, that wouldn't necessarily cause havoc. If she's in her office, it might not be that hard to terminate her quietly; and really that's a better way to go."

The manicured statue that was my brother supplied, "She's in there every morning and she thinks I'm a perfect model citizen. It should be pretty easy for me to get in there to give her a report on the new inmates."

I almost laughed at the joke I could make about being a male model citizen. Then again, I was looking at my stone faced sibling. "So you're going to go up to the third floor and break her neck with karate?" My brother began nodding his head. "And then you're going back to the ground floor to karate this other guy?"

His nod came to a crawl as he said, "Neither should take much time."

I shrugged. Perhaps it didn't take that long to kill a person with a well placed chop. Maybe cracking someone's spine was as simple as a Vulcan neck pinch.

I wanted some full sleeves on my skinny arms tomorrow in case we ended up running through the woods. We were in a zombie apocalypse but I was still worried about briars and shit. I looked through Easy's footlocker and found the closest approximation to long sleeves I could realistically wear: a grotesquely large short sleeve polo shirt. We were nearly the same height; I didn't realize my bodybuilder brother had a wardrobe designed for Mighty Joe Young. Shit, Smokes could fit his entire body through one of the arms! I would have to tie rubber bands around each wrist. I could probably get by without wearing pants as long as there was no breeze. I reckon it could be worse, it could smell like Easy's cologne. It did have the faintest hint of cocoa butter lotion.

Aka noticed my rummaging. She graciously decided to come help the deviant that was her future brother-in-law. After some discussion, I held up the hopelessly large shirt that I had picked out. She scoffed and stepped to her own footlocker and pulled out a piece of clothing. She returned with a black scrub top and a smile. Thank God it wasn't pink or covered in rainbow kittens. I slipped it on over my shirt just to make sure it fit. Plus, I wanted to smell like lavender. This African princess was fairly tall for a female. I would like to say that it fit pretty tight around my biceps. You know, because I'm so muscular.

Zombies On A Plane

    I'm not going to think about how it affects my "man score" to be able to fit into my brother's fiancée's clothes. I simply thanked her as I folded the shirt in my hand and returned to the COUCH.

Javan Bonds

Interlude 3

As I reached my seat, I could hear my brother continuing his list of complaints to the general group about how the prison was not a lavish five-star resort. "And the toilet paper is another thing; it's only one ply!"

This is the most sissified thing for any male to bitch about. Do you hear men crying in the stalls at Walmart or pulling out feminine napkins because they can't bare the scrape against their sensitive anus? I actually prefer one ply compared to your six ply toilet tissue. It's cheaper and doesn't fill up a septic tank as fast. I don't think anyone can take Sheryl Crow's advice of only using a single square per dump with one ply, but it's certainly more economical. I nearly retorted, "One-ply don't bother me, my asshole ain't as sensitive as your lady parts!" but decided to keep my mouth shut after I thought about it. I might as well have added, "My boyfriend Lance made sure of that."

I now feel less masculine for thinking I'm more masculine for not being prissy than I did when I fit perfectly into clothing designed for a woman.

The radio chimed. "Mo, this is Gray Fox, do you read?"

I was thankful he interrupted Easy's whining about the thread counts of the sheets and that he asked for me I replied, "We got you, Daddy. What's up?"

He sighed before coming back, "Well, a lot. I will summarize. Dr. George's Phantoms are going out tonight to capture a peevie. We have a PT boat. Now that–"

My testosterone overdosed sibling interrupted, "Like in *Apocalypse Now*? Sweet!

"It's really only a bass boat with a machine gun mounted to the deck, but, yeah, it's pretty much the same thing."

I'm sure my brother intended to ask him to text over some pictures. He would then realize the prison staff had confiscated his iPhone, which would likely send him into another bitch fest. He would completely ignore the fact that he wouldn't be getting any service after armageddon.

Zombies On A Plane

Compare it to my father discussing the monetary worth of comic books a few weeks ago with The Tech or Hammer's delusional driving etiquette. The world has gone mad.

"So y'all got a plan for getting out of there?" I was proud he decided I was useful and would be in the middle of the strategic committee.

I started detailing our plan of escape to my father. I was constantly interrupted by the entire delegation.

"And then I'll go down to deal with the guard."

"We'll use He-Man's face scrubs as an accelerant."

"I'll lay down cover fire."

"I'll keep the guard busy."

"Den I'm a fly dese peoples back."

He waited until he received only silence, then my father came back, "Well that sounds pretty in-depth. I'm not there so I can't really suggest anything. Just give me a buzz when you get to the plane."

This plan had nearly as many holes as did our first leisurely stroll through no man's land for condiments. You could also compare it to our severely retarded decision to casually enter a Walmart that could have been teaming with sexually deprived sadists. Our earlier journeys through hell had amazingly worked out, so my dad was clearly putting his trust in The Oracle. Trusting the lives of his children to a drug dealer that would sell our souls for a Twinkie. Putting his faith in a person that was willing to risk more than one life for ketchup, believing we were safe if The Oracle approved of our plan. Let me reiterate again, he was willing to accept a poorly thought escape and decided his offspring could not be harmed because a guy with marijuana leaf decals on his purple Escalade was with us! I feel so loved.

Mama could be heard approaching the other end of the radio to say a few things to us. Does it really surprise you that she was eager to speak to us on our second and third night only after Easy was found?

Anyway, she was heard coming into the room, excited. She was moving closer, "Oh, let me talk to–" just then she belted out a deafening banshee scream. She continued as if she had not just nearly brown-noted every person within a mile radius. "Them."

Zombies On A Plane

My eyes grew wide, initially fearing it was the last exclamation of a person stabbed repeatedly, though I knew what it was, a normal occurrence in the Collins home…she sneezed. Whenever I sneeze, everyone around me has several seconds warning and I have to hold on to something or I will blow myself over. I remember sitting in English class in high school and turning my head to sneeze, it hit Jenna in the face on the other side of the room, proving I'm a mouth-sneezer. But Easy is just as guilty as our mother. You could be in the middle of a conversation with them and they give no warning; their speech just suddenly explodes with a sound similar to that of a cat being run over by a speeding lawnmower. I'm just thankful my dad was only a year or two too young to have been drafted in Vietnam, otherwise my mother's sneezes would surely trigger Agent Orange flashbacks and we would have all been murdered more than once years ago.

I know he jumped; everyone does when she sneezes like that, but I didn't hear him fall to the floor dead from a heart attack. She hadn't actually managed to scare the life out of him yet. He handed over the radio and she began with her usual motherly questions.

I had not expected my brother to give her the full story on Aka, how they were engaged, that is, but he did. Of course my mother was thrilled and couldn't wait to meet her future daughter-in-law. We made sure to inform my dad that my brother's Zambian fiancée was confident she could run a hydroelectric dam, or at least switch it on. He surely thought it was divine providence foretold by Smokes and handed to us by George Romero or something.

He casually hinted that we had come to the end of our conversation. He was clearly not worried that we could be riddled with bullets or raped by peevies by this time tomorrow. "Well, those special forces fellas should be headed out here soon and the doc ought to be calling, so…"

I picked up. "All right, Daddy. I'll give you a buzz tomorrow when we make it to the plane. Tell Mama and Sarah–"

My perfect brother loudly interrupted, "I love you, Mama!"

Dammit, he has always loved to steal my thunder. I might have asked to speak to Sarah; this would have been a perfect time to finally admit my undying, romantic love for her but he just beat down my opportunity. I could be horribly maimed and killed tomorrow. What if this is the last conversation I will ever have with my parents? My last transmission was interrupted by my polar opposite sibling.

"Ha ha…she heard you, son. Gray Fox out."

Thanks, EASY!

Javan Bonds

27

Treachery

BOBBITT SEEMED WILLING to go at Earl's pace, which was fine with The Betrayer, though he was almost shocked that the military man was not falling over himself to get on the island before they got more organized with their defenses. Right now they were ripe for the picking.

Earl spent all day detailing the movements of the guards on the South Causeway, fishing and working in several of the community gardens so that he could eat. This was not some type of hippie commune where everything was free; if you ate out of the community pot, you contributed. He didn't mind that; earning what you got was how the world worked, in general. This sanctuary would actually be an okay place to live if that redheaded cunt was not one of the bosses. He had learned that the evil lesbo was the town sheriff, but was currently on indefinite leave. He was hoping she'd get back in time for him to personally slit her throat.

He had looked around Bottom Dollar and decided that the building was buttoned up pretty tight, no easy way to break in. Burning that place to the ground wasn't really a priority and he would shed no tears, it wasn't a big deal. If Hammer was here, he would make sure to burn the place down with her alive inside, but for now he had to focus on the bridge guards.

It was nearing the end of his second day of "looking for a job" to become a productive member of society. Earl sat on the Best Western dock and dropped a un-baited hook into the water, watching the sun set behind the mountains. It took hours for everything to die down. Even with such a small population, the island seemed to be as active as a pre-apocalypse city. Finally, the only sound that could be heard was the occasional laugh or cough from the two men on the bridge. Just as he had practiced, he crouched along the shoreline and stayed on the outer edge of the causeway, the aluminum railing between him and the road. Earl made sure to keep his feet from crunching on the loose gravel.

When The Betrayer neared the gap in the causeway, where he was basically even with the guard shack on the other side of the railing, he sat down to wait as he came to the waterline.

Zombies On A Plane

He knew that eventually, one of the two armored men would need to take a piss break. The former truck driver had originally considered acting injured at the end of the causeway and calling for help. That idea was discarded because it would be two on one and they always wore their helmets outside of the shack. This practice was so routine for them, he only knew that they were un-helmeted inside the shack because he had seen them snapping their head covers as they exited.

With one suit of armor taking a leak and probably without a walkie-talkie, Earl could sneak into the shack, terminate the unsuspecting astronaut, silently and quickly. Even if his buddy was alerted, he could not radio for backup and wouldn't likely go running with his dick hanging out. It had to take some time to get everything back into one of those suits. The radios inside the small building buzzed and a short conversation could be heard.

An Indian voice sounded over the radio. "This is Foxtrot Niner Mike. Humvee approaching South Causeway. Please bridge the gap so we may cross. Out."

One of the soldiers called back, "Roger Roger."

One man exited the guard shack and walked across the pavement. This might be his chance. He began to breathe deeply as he readied his knife. The armored guard jumped the rail to get to the jet ski.

The heavy boots landed on the gravel on the other side of the causeway. Earl quickly slid closer to the water in case he needed to escape. The Betrayer heard the jet-ski start and nearly shit his pants.

Are they really bridging the gap now? Crap! Earl had no idea what was happening. He lowered himself into the water without a sound. The jet ski came through the gap and turned to stop just beyond him. The former truck driver willed himself into invisibility as the guard killed the engine. Head just above the water, Earl could hear the rumble of an approaching vehicle.

He watched as a boxy automobile zoomed by, bounced across the pontoon bridge, and disappeared into the night. He could do nothing but guess what reason anyone would have to go out at night unless they were looking for trouble. He was so completely deep in thought he did not even register the guard pulling the pontoon away from the road, stopping the jet-ski again, and jumping back to land.

Earl was shaken from his stupor as the two watchmen broke into conversation inside the guard shack. He mentally kicked himself for being so easily distracted, trying to push theories and ideas of why anyone would willingly leave the island at night from his mind.

All he had to do now was wait for some of that instant coffee he knew the guards were drinking to take effect. Eventually, one of them would be making a pit stop.

Finally the guard armored in white snapped his helmet on as he hustled to the edge of the causeway and started fumbling with his crotch. The former truck driver smiled as he quietly hefted himself over the railing and onto the pavement. He knew that all men felt that pain and had at one point, for one reason or another, had the same battle with their zippers. He crouched, drawing his large knife as he peeked into the surprisingly well-lit guard shack to see that, thankfully, the soldier in red armor was facing the rear of the building. The man was apparently shuffling a deck of cards.

As he took a crouched step towards the guard, a board creaked under his foot. The guard assumed his compatriot had returned. He called without turning, "Did you find it? I figured out that you can leave the top buckle fastened when–" Earl ended the man's explanation with a cupped hand over his mouth and a Bowie knife across his throat.

Dark red blood coated the inside of the shack, spraying like a faucet from the open aorta. The man went slack; Earl let the body slump to the floor as his life spilled down the front of his suit. Even before the body stopped pouring blood everywhere, Earl began stripping the warm corpse of its red armor. As he suited up, The Betrayer found it funny; the sticky fluid was clearly visible against the Crimson steel.

"Got your helmet on, huh?" questioned the returning guard. He unsnapped his own as he made his way around the table.

This unobservant fuck didn't even notice his blood soaked comrade crumpled in the corner to his right. *He deserves what I'm about to do to him.* Earl turned to face the un-helmeted guard, whose eyes grew wide. Before noticing the knife, he asked the helmeted figure, "Lee! Are you bleeding or something?"

The Betrayer took a step forward and slashed the standing guard's throat open with one quick motion. The razor sharp blade split his throat with no resistance. The guard could do nothing but gurgle as he collapsed and clutched at his throat. Rapidly flowing crimson slowed along with his heartbeat.

Zombies On A Plane

Earl was amazed at how easy it all was; it had to be fate that they were meant to take over the island. That stupid bitch deserved to feel a real man give it to her before she was disemboweled. She was going to have a hell of a "welcome home" surprise.

The walkie-talkie lay on the table behind him. It buzzed with what sounded like a Quickie Mart employee. "This is Foxtrot Niner, Mike. We have completed our current mission and are returning to the island. Please bring the bridge around. Over."

Shit, Earl thought. *I hate to give the defenders even more troops, but I don't want to set off any alarms by ignoring the call.* He uncovered his face and spoke quickly into the radio, "Roger Roger! Out." Earl dropped his helmet back down and hurried outside to move the pontoon attached to the jet-ski. Once the vehicle had bounced onto the island side, he left the gap bridged.

Now he didn't feel rushed and sauntered back to the guardhouse. The Betrayer casually informed the captain of his progress. "Hey, Bobbitt, the way's clear whenever you feel like coming."

They had discussed that the main attack would not begin until sunrise. For obvious reasons, he wasn't in a rush. With confirmation from the other end of the radio, Earl headed to his next objective.

If any peevies were to wander across the connecting bridge, it could only help by adding to the chaos he was hoping to create. Earl had also discussed this part of the plan with the captain; without the mayor, the Islanders would have even more trouble rallying. Cut the dumbass hillbilly head off the snake and the rest of it will be pretty easy to take down. Treachery was Earl Buckalew's favorite sin–it always paid OFF.

28

Under Observation

"THE BRIDGE WAS in place as we reached it so we just slowed down and bounced on over," The Phantom began his report. "We drove a few hundred meters past the mouth of the causeway and found the designated spot in the gas bank parking lot. The Humvee stopped in the corner of the lot and we were met by complete silence. The young bull put up no struggle as I walked it a distance in front of the vehicle's lights, luring the animal with a large container of feed. I secured the bull to a light pole and stepped back to watch and wait."

The man cleared his throat and looked at his teammates. "Mahatma manned the mounted 50, Rajesh and I watched the flanks with our rifles, and Sanjay waited with a net gun. Animal howls and shrieks could be heard intensifying as the predators drew closer; these sounds were obviously not from coyotes or other identifiable local fauna.

Figures began to appear in my night vision monocular; definitely bipedal. We confirmed them as our targets. They became progressively aroused as they drew closer to fresh prey."

He paused to control a shudder, swallowing hard. "It was more than a little frightening to watch animals, beasts, that had been people not that long ago snarling, hissing, and growling as they formed a semicircle around the calf. The squad decided via radio that our subject for capture would be a small male, a child, near the far left of the line. With a final radio click, Mahatma began opening fire from right to left, mowing down the infected as they barked and screamed in confusion."

The Phantom closed his eyes, remembering the slaughter, but continued his report."Rajesh flipped the headlights on; the infected were so driven by bloodlust and hunger that they attempted to dodge the flying bullets and continued to press forward to their meal. The dozen or so had quickly been cut down to three, and we began hammering the two others with small arms fire. Sanjay simultaneously lined up to trap our chosen afflicted. The former human, err, boy, lunged for the defenseless bovine, getting its last meal before being imprisoned."

He looked at the ground, considered his words, then continued. "It was a terrible waste, but the risk of spreading sickness through tainted meat was too great. I put a single bullet through the calf's brain. Three of us quickly exited the vehicle and began the tedious task of getting the entangled plague victim into the back of the Humvee."

Randy guessed this had to be Kumar. It actually wasn't entirely impossible to tell The Phantoms apart after spending some time around them. "Well," he said, "I'm just glad none of y'all got hurt and got back with the peevie. Where's it at?"

The hit gestured, "Follow me, it's sedated and secured."

The mayor wasn't afraid for his own safety, but he knew to be cautious. As he walked down the hall, he thought about how he had just seen one zombie cause the destruction of more than one supposedly safe community in way too many movies.

The door flew open and the mayor immediately double-checked. "It's tied down and sedated right?"

Dr. George smiled, "And there are four operators with assault rifles at the ready." The Medicine Man was confident that there was no chance their subject would make it out of this room. Even though the confidence of millions of others in history and fiction had led to their demise, he was sure this thing could go nowhere.

A pale blue, filthy, completely naked young man lay strapped to the table before them. Every person in the room could barely tear their eyes from the form, you could compare them to children in a biology lab intently studying a live insect with a pin through it. The blue tint to its skin appeared almost gray, and Randy nearly asked if that was normal for all of them. He silently chuckled. Being from Alabama he compared this to a blue cow; upon closer inspection it was easy to see that the cow was not actually blue but grayish.

The doctor had it hooked up to an EKG machine and was monitoring its other vitals. He had already taken a urine sample for testing; being out in the elements, it had to be full of infections. Lying quietly, it appeared to be nothing more than a bluish teenage boy. But the team all knew that they could not make the mistake of thinking of this monster as an innocent, diseased human.

Zombies On A Plane

The pulse was somewhat erratic, but living outside on a diet of raw meat could cause this; the cardiologist saw no need to worry about its immediate demise. Even the genitalia appeared completely normal besides the discoloration. He tried to push thoughts of dissection from his mind, he needed a living research subject for as long as possible.

Randy wasn't really sure what to do. He asked, "So what now?"

"We will keep this room blocked off and I will do some tests with UV light when it wakes up. I can devise useful tests to perform on it for the rest of its life."

"Do you think you can get a cure or vaccine or something out of it?"

The cardiologist frowned. "We haven't seen enough yet to know what the disease even is. I am not too hopeful for a cure for those already infected, though. A resistant antivirus to prevent further infections might be a possibility. When this particular subject is no longer functioning, I will be able to dissect the cardiac muscle and will be closer to my answer."

"Well I'm glad you called me to come see it. I better go before the Misses locks me out of the house again."

His cheek twitched when he realized that he had referred to the county courthouse as "home" yet again. The mayor pointed in the general direction of the other Phantoms as he stood. "One of your boys already filled me in on its capture. I'll let you get to it." Mayor Collins waved as he turned to walk out of the room.

Dr. George was reading over an EKG report. He spoke to the mayor's back without looking up, "I will be sure to let you know of any developments."

The mayor nodded and contemplated a possible vaccine as he walked to his vehicle. He could see humans rising to the top of the food chain once MORE.

28

Chief Engineer Gene Stanley's Log 3

I KNOW IT'S near midnight, darker than a Minoc's cave. This day has been packed with more work than any twenty-five hour Sera day should be. We finally got our first fast attack boat completed and can hopefully construct more in coming cycles. Maybe next I'll try for a Halo Warthog or a Tie Fighter.

Hunter broke his arm today and really required as much comforting as would a troll, that is to say absolutely none. His mother was unbelievably devastated, spending more time blaming a person that is hundreds of miles away for a simple accident than the time Luke spent studying the Force. I am going to have to warn her that simply drinking her anger down is only leading her down a dark path. 'Darth Georgia' does not sound catchy; plus, black is not her color.

I just got off the horn with the mayor and he bid me come to the courthouse in the morning. I believe, he has something to show me. It's not my birthday, so I don't know if I should be expecting a Marty McFly skateboard or a surprise like Joe Pesci's in *Goodfellas*.

I think I just heard Georgia call me. I'll continue this entry when I get back. Alas, the trials of being in a committed relationship with an insanely attractive PRINCESS.

29

Violence

EARL WALKED AND jogged for what seemed like hours in the direction of the courthouse. He was completely unimpeded and met nothing but the hum of the occasional gas powered generator for most of his trek. Suddenly a pair of headlights came into view; he jogged over to the ditch and lay down. The vehicle finally passed by leaving him undetected, free to continue his journey. Who could that have been? The tail lights appeared to turn, they were definitely not going to the causeway. At least, not yet.

If everything was black and white I would think this was fucking Mayberry, he thought. *They might as well roll up the damn streets at night.* He knew that this city'd had a nightlife pre-Armageddon, but now there wasn't anything happening. It was like only senior citizens survived.

As he came to within a few blocks of his intended target, The Betrayer was verbally accosted by a clearly drunken female voice. "What the fuck are you doing, soldier?"

Holy shit, he almost swallowed his tongue. A human voice was the one thing he didn't want to hear. He looked over to see a blonde girl sitting on the road, leaning back against the curb. She clutched a half-empty bottle of Early Times in her hand. Damn, this girl drank some manly whiskey. He was taking her full form in from top to bottom, admiring every curve. She had a perfect rack that was close to falling out of her tank top. This hot piece of ass was unsuccessfully hiding those gorgeous legs under what Daisy Duke could barely consider shorts.

He had clipped the helmet to the leg of his spacesuit, she could see the look on his face as he checked her out. She rose and began seductively walking towards him. "You want some of this big boy?" She smacked her ass as she drew up to him, "Well, let's just walk on in here to where my tall, dark boyfriend is and we can–" her humor instantly turned to horror. "Are you bleeding? What the fuck?" Because the armor was red, she had not noticed the drying blood covering the front until she got close.

The drunken woman turned back to the closest building. "Gene? Gene! There's one of the storm trooper guys out here and–"

Earl gripped her arm and pulled her to him. He tried to keep his voice barely above a whisper. "Shut the fuck up, bitch!" This was not part of his plan and he had to improvise. "This was all a dream and you never saw me."

He intended to render her unconscious by knocking her in the head and figured he would get a handful as he reached up. *Damned armored gloves!* She let out a bloodcurdling scream as his hand moved up. She tried to pull away from the freak as he pulled her closer. Quickly sobering up, Georgia desperately struggled to get away from this creep before he could really hurt her.

The Betrayer pulled the knife from the sheath attached to his rifle's shoulder strap and attempted to scare her into silence. "Be quiet, you stupid cunt." He smiled as she began futilely kicking his armored crotch. "Or we can have some fun with Mr. Bowie."

The little bitch had some balls, still fighting like mad. His scare tactic obviously didn't work. She was somehow still holding onto the bottle and brought it around and hit him across the face

Earl was surprised that the thick glass bottle simply shattered on impact rather than cracking his jaw. He had seen those things thrown into stop signs while driving ninety miles an hour down the road, they would just bounce off.

Now bleeding from multiple lacerations on his face, he was so angry that he jammed his knife to the hilt up under her ribcage. Soft squishing sounds could be heard as he drove the dagger deep into her chest, slicing open at least a lung. He gently shushed her and grabbed at her breasts as he lowered her to the pavement.

He slowly stood and backed away from the fading girl he had just murdered. He could hear an exclamation from the door of the building, "Georgia! The nerdy-looking man fixed his gaze on Earl. "What did you do, you son of a bantha?"

The thin figure began approaching Earl. The armored man then brought his rifle to bear. Before Gene could react and before Earl could pull the trigger, The Betrayer was suddenly beheaded. The man's skull seem to vaporize, gray matter exploding and blood shooting like a fountain from the neck as the armor collapsed. It took a second for Gene to hear the report of the shot that dropped the man who murdered his lover. The Betrayer's violence had finally brought him to his end.

Zombies On A Plane

The tech was incredulous. He asked the man holding the rifle standing a few hundred yards behind where the headless body now lay, "Randy? Why aren't you at the courthouse?"

The mayor walked closer and kicked the orb-less armor. "The doc has a peevie sedated in the clinic and he called me to come see it. I was just on my way back and this space marine must not have heard my Humvee."

Gene cocked his head, briefly wondering how the older man knew of the suit's universe of origin. "Who is– was he?"

"Hell if I know, I doubt we'll find any of his teeth." the mayor joked on dental records. A light bulb came on over Mayor Collins's head. "Which causeway was this armor supposed to be at?"

The Tech had to think before replying. "The Blood Raven was at the south. Why?"

Gene slowly came to the realization as Mayor Collins lifted his radio. "Doc, emergency! Get The Phantoms to the southern causeway ASAP!"

As the mayor ran back to his vehicle he turned to the shocked engineer, still clad in his *Transformers* pajamas. He offered sympathetically, "I'm sorry I can't stay. And sorry about Georgia. Wish there was something I could do!"

Randy did a U-turn and sped off into the night, leaving Gene alone in complete silence and utter shock. He could not decide if he had just flow walked (a Jedi time travel ability) at warp nine or if any of this was real. He had to go back and think how he got to this point at this moment. When he and Georgia had returned with Hunter earlier tonight–that was already last night now– she kept blaming Smokes for all of her troubles and retrieved something that she said was Daniel's, a half-gallon of bourbon. She stayed outside to drown her sorrows, Gene let her have her time. He had only been alerted a few minutes ago when she called for him. Had someone killed a bridge guard, stolen his uniform, and walked on foot all this way just to assassinate the woman of his dreams? The killer did not appear to be bald or have a barcode on the back of his head, when he had a head, so Gene was clueless. Georgia was dead, he was confident of this. He knew there was no reason to check for a pulse on her cooling form.

Zombies On A Plane

"There is no emotion, there is peace. There is no ignorance, there is knowledge. There is no passion, there is serenity. There is no chaos, there is harmony. There is no death, there is the Force." He calmed himself while repeating the Jedi code like a mantra. He knelt beside her still body. His was quivering inside like gelatin. But he had to remain serene, at least until he figured out what was going on.

As he grasped her pale hand, thoughts of his Mother flashed across his mind. He had lost the two most important women in his life within a month of each other. He made a promise to her stiffening form and to himself that he would take care of Hunter as if he were his own. This loss would haunt him for the rest of his life, but he did not have the luxury to fall apart. If the island was being attacked the needs of the many outweighed the needs of the few, or the ONE.

Javan Bonds

30

Mo Journal Entry 12

I HAVE APPARENTLY grown accustomed to my torturous daily schedule of waking before sunrise. I blinked my eyes open right as the one eyed slave driver returned from the bathroom.

She stood there, completely suited up and ready for a glorious death. The labor boss looked over her victims of the day, determining the level of physical abuse each of us could withstand. She noticed that I was looking at her and The Expert cut her eye at me. Her drill instructor bellow grew in earth shattering intensity with each syllable, "Why are you still in the bed? Get up and get dressed! Sunrise is in three minutes!"

God Almighty, take it easy lady. I ain't even took my morning piss yet. I rose, walked into the bathroom, and I'm not sorry I got it all over the seat that I didn't raise and probably the floor. I was out in what was record time for me in my black scrub top and bullet proof vest, feeling as manly as any male can sporting women's apparel.

Hammer had obviously rudely awakened the entire group, including my barely functional brother and his fiancée, while I was getting dressed. They were both wiping their eyes as the couple accepted caffeine pills from the expert. I don't think I could've ingested contraband offered by her, God knows where she's been hiding it for the past two days. I probably shouldn't bring that up to Easy, he's one of those people who refuses to get out of bed before noon, he needed the caffeine to keep him alert enough to not fall asleep as we ran to the plane. He was functioning, but I knew he would make sure everyone knew he wasn't enjoying being awake at a decent hour. By all means, I enjoy my sleep, but I'm more of a morning person, at least after a cup of coffee. Hammer must have decided that more than six hours of rest is for lazy people. She nearly made Smokes cry as she screamed at him to hurry up.

Zombies On A Plane

"Shit white lady, you can't rush summin' so beautiful." I wasn't gonna think about what he could be implying as he sighed, grunted, and moaned in relief. It sounded like a weird porn movie I had seen before. "Dat's ova now, hos." I shuddered, picturing a darker version of Fat Bastard from Austin Powers lamenting, "I didn't eat corn!"

I stowed the walkie-talkie almost hidden in the armor, it was on my chest, close enough that I would be able to hear the chime just in case it was to buzz. Even so, I wasn't expecting any calls. I would either need to call my dad and tell him we were on our way or at least send a final message as I fall under a rain of bullets. I questioned The Oracle, "So we got everything we need, right?"

The assembled group nodded their readiness. It was clear that most of them were working themselves up mentally for what was coming. The Expert felt at her pocket of grenades before answering, "Looks like it. Those KGB hippies won't know what hit 'em." She stopped before being the first out of the door and turned to the lovers. To reassure the unarmored pair, she added: "I'm sure we'll find some extra vests in the armory. You will have some protection before we start our run."

Our band moved in the general direction of the cafeteria. We slunk into the large building to our left. This was the administration building where everything would go down before our escape. Once inside, Hammer communicated to us through hand signals. She gestured for my brother to move upstairs, Aka to go find that desperate guard, Tychus to accompany her to one of the upper floors, and I was to lead Smokes by grabbing his shoulder. The two of us were to wait near the armory. I really need to get Hammer to go over the meaning of hand signals with my overly large friend. Perhaps she could teach a class on tactical movements when we get back to the island. That class would immediately follow her lessons in Soviet Slaying 101. Of course, it would lead up to Crow's home economics lessons on cooking bland, unseasoned fish. Gene should have a class on mechanical engineering or something. I might have a weekly seminar on how to be a worthless jackass, if I feel like it.

We watched from around the corner as the African princess pleaded with the guard. I nearly laughed at her suggestions about "touching big guns." The cop shakily fumbled to get his key into the lock as the blood rushed away from his cranium.

Zombies On A Plane

I could clearly understand his frustration and sympathize, a piece of literal chocolate was being bounced in front of him and he was starving. Any heterosexual man with a penis would be having the same problem.

It looked like he was about to start crying at his inability to find the key. If something didn't happen soon, I was afraid he might burst into flames. I got a tap on my shoulder and almost screamed. "The warden is done," Easy whispered.

I snickered, "Done? How long did you put her in the microwave?"

He deadpanned questioningly, "No. I mean she was taken care of."

He didn't even seem shaken up, I was actually proud of my brother. I mean, killing a person with your bare hands is pretty badass in itself, but he did not seem phased that he had just broken a human's neck. I've only killed peevies to this date; I don't think I would want to be in Easy's shoes. Hell, I might be found later, crying in the fetal position because I took a life. I like to think I'm as big a man as my younger brother.

Javan Bonds

I'm not one of those perverts that gets off on those stories about men brutalizing women, but I had to have the gory details in case I ever needed to murder someone with my excessive STRENGTH.

31

Bound

Prophecy from *The Book of Smokes:*

The Protector is calm, does not tend to show deep emotions, and may even appear dimwitted to some. When the need arises and other main protagonists are in jeopardy, the character will seem to transform into a lunatic berserker. The Protector will always defend those that cannot defend themselves. Will never start the fight, but always makes sure it gets finished.

He rapped his knuckles on the door. "It's open," could be heard from the other side. Easy closed the door behind him as he walked to the desk. Warden Slice faced him from the opposite side, her gaze warm for her favorite detainee.

After the niceties were out of the way she got down to business. "How is everything going with our new citizens?" The Dictator continued, "Are they acclimating well to our command structure?"

A look of worry crossed her face as The Protector exhaled with a hint of sadness. He answered, "Well, that's what I came here to talk to you about."

She stood and turned to face the window. She watched as loyal citizens filed into the cafeteria before starting their daily chores. "They are not content to be safe?"

"I don't think they like being forced to stay here," he began from his seat on the other side of the desk. She gasped, spinning around to face him with her hands still behind her back. He was nearly on top of her in the blink of an eye. "And neither do I."

The bodybuilder slammed his full weight into her, crashing her back into the floor-to-ceiling window. Her skull bounced off the bulletproof glass and her eyes simultaneously closed. He was thankful the glass was one-way, mirrored on the other side. If anyone had seen what he'd done, he would already have been swarmed by guards. The Protector really didn't want to be on the wrong side of a hostage situation using the unconscious warden as a shield.

Zombies On A Plane

He was just as thankful the glass was thick. Not that he would've been brokenhearted if she fell out of the building, but someone may have noticed it was raining humans.

She was out cold and now he had to think on what to do with her. While strategizing with his brother's crew, he had intended to kill the warden. The Protector had just acted spontaneously upon entering the room. Now the younger Collins was not sure he was psychologically prepared to murder a helpless and unconscious person. Maybe he could just put her out of action for the foreseeable future. In her desk, he found a few zip ties and enough tape to keep her quiet for a while. He looked around the room for a place to stow her concussed form. *"That'll Work!"* He zip-tied her hands and feet before taping her mouth shut, she wouldn't be going anywhere at least for the rest of the day. The bodybuilder lifter her, throwing her arms over the moose rack, satisfied her arms would be sore when she woke. Easy opened the door, locked it, and then broke said lock before heading downstairs so no one could enter and find the WARDEN.

Javan Bonds

32

The Game Changer

THE DOCTOR THOUGHT he should run some quick tests on the captured plague victim; no time like the present. He would be able to handle it himself, even with the other phantoms away dealing with a dispute or whatever it was. The Medicine Man would've accompanied them to meet the mayor at the southern causeway, but felt that immediate study of this new subject was more important. The Phantoms would be able to handle any domestic disturbance. The cardiologist was more intent on gaining any information concerning the infection as soon as possible.

During his first testing with chemicals, he discovered that the infected was driven insanely hungry by a very small amount of vinegar. Though it did not physically injure the creature, he found that it reacted to trace amounts of alcohol as if it caused a burning sensation. No other liquid provided any reaction.

Dr. George was ready for more. He went to retrieve several items for use in experiments. As he opened the door, light from the barest hint of the sunrise crossed over the plague victim. The cardiologist was surprised there were no screams or howls, no signs of distress. Dr. George got a new idea. Even if it might bring expiration earlier than expected, he was willing to put the subject under more stressful tests. If it was terminated, that would simply mean he could start studying its infected heart sooner. The doctor knew it all sounded cruel and that some would cry that "peevies are people too!" He was more concerned with the rights of thinking humans and would do everything he could to get closer to ending the danger posed by these monsters and whatever was affecting them.

The Medicine Man reentered the room with a cart of various bulbs and lighting equipment. He flipped on a battery-powered neon light but got no response. The thing had not noticed the room's incandescent bulbs or his battery-powered penlight. The Phantom doctor still had a few more to try. A cigarette lighter, florescent bulb, and LED fixture also produced nothing. He finally flipped on a UV light and pointed it straight at the animal, completely strapped down on the gurney.

It blinked; but nothing out of the ordinary. After again receiving little reaction when he had definitely expected something, he lowered the electric light and pulled the cover off of the window in the door. Natural sunlight shone directly on the thing's face but it still didn't seem to care. Its pupils were visibly dilated, dark yellow openings centered in bright yellow eyes irises and surrounded by pale yellow sclera, disgusting, but human-like–not feline as he had noted before..

The Medicine Man lifted his walkie-talkie. He spoke breathlessly and shakily, "Randy, I think we might need to look out for some new DEVELOPMENTS."

33

Mo Journal Entry 13

I TURNED, WATCHING and waiting for my brother to enter the scene unfolding in the armory. I finally turned back to see Easy just standing there with a perplexed look on his face. "Fucking go" I mouthed. I gestured intently in the direction of his fiancée. I agreed with The Expert that we should go get our needed weapons before the grenades went off upstairs. We were kind of on a strict time schedule, the dumbass needed to get a move on.

He moved much too silently for someone of his size. I could compare it to The Oracle's raccoon slippers or maybe it was his use of the Force–neither would know what I was talking about there. It seemed he had simply appeared just outside the door, waiting to throw himself around the corner.

Aka nearly had Mr. Rent-a-Cop passed out from blood loss. That would kinda be a less painful way to go for him.

She bent over in front of him to pick something up and I almost broke out in a sweat. He had his back to us, but I'm not sure it would have mattered if Easy had started screaming like a madman at the other end of the hall. He was too entranced to notice anything beyond the bootylicious treat before him.

My brother punched the security guard in the temple, his stadium -style class ring audibly impacting against bone. The small man collapsed on his side, a neatly folded piece of luggage. The Oracle and I moved up even with the white Incredible Hulk.

My brother's fiancée began in her normally soft voice, "Thank God! I'm not sure how much more of that I could have taken…"

"Yeah, me either," I stated matter-of-factly. I received humorless silence from the audience. Even Smokes gave me a look of disgust. Like he wasn't enjoying the show!

My brother shut the door and dragged the limp body to a storage locker. He was able to force the unconscious little man inside before breaking the lock. It seemed like he had done this before, shoving kids into lockers. I chose not to comment from the peanut gallery of critics.

Zombies On A Plane

My future sister-in-law found some bulletproof vests in an orderly pile. She slipped one over her head before tossing one to Easy. I was sure that even if it was a one-size-fits-all vest, it would come nowhere close to covering his giant body. I was confused when he slipped it on and smoothed it out to fit perfectly over is muscular chest. What the hell? That was as impossible as The Oracle's fitting into his vest with room to spare at Bottom Dollar on the day we met Hammer.

We all began shoving pistols into our waistbands and throwing rifles over our shoulders. We were confident each was loaded after discovering the first few miraculously contained ammunition. Do all prisons keep loaded firearms inside? That doesn't seem safe. Maybe it's all part of the plan.

Before leaving the room, I discovered something that might help us make our prison break: cartons of grenades. Hammer would probably orgasm. I'm a little disappointed there were no RPGs.

We exited the room at a slow pace, over-encumbered by countless weapons. Maybe we would find a magic bag on our way or simply drop most of them once we got to our designated meeting point of the rear fire exit. We could even stumble upon a merchant who would pay for some of our wares.

Javan Bonds

While I'm waxing *Never Winter Nights*, I'll go ahead and choose to be a cleric/fighter Dwarf named HANNIBAL.

34

Not A Killing Shot

THEY BRIEFLY SCOUTED the two upper floors and came to a mutual decision. Hammer would start by dropping a grenade in the middle of the office space on the top floor. The two would rush to the stairway on the opposite side of the floor where The Loner would ready his grenade. They would descend to the next office where he would lay his explosive, then they would head to the ground floor. This would be easy as pie. They were sure any guards they ran into while descending would assume they were merely among the scant few office workers left after May first, rushing to escape the unexplained explosions above.

On the second floor, the janitor held the grenade and slowed near the middle of the long hallway that ran across the level. He pulled the pin, about to drop the explosive as they hustled. Hammer was a few feet ahead of him as an armed security guard came around the corner.

The guard's eyes focused on The Loner, alert at the sight of the grenade. He drew his pistol as he screamed, "What the fuck are you doing–" His question was then wrapped by a stiff running kick between his legs courtesy of The Expert. As he dropped to his knees, he was able to get two wild shots off in the direction of the elderly black man. One of the poorly aimed shots took out Adjutant, immediately killing the poor animal and sending him flying off the janitor's shoulder. The second shot hit what was soon to be The Sacrifice, our second one, below the knee.

The Loner momentarily collapsed while still squeezing the spoon of the frag. Captain Sledge thrust the heel of her boot into the guard's face, preventing another shot. Already on the floor due to her nut shot, the unconscious man now simply looked like he was sleeping. She moved back, realizing her comrade had only been shot in the center of his right calf, far from being a fatal wound. Hammer helped him to his feet and began half carrying him as he dropped his grenade. He might likely survive such a gunshot wound; The Expert had taken much worse herself. But Hammer could not fool herself; the Captain already knew the score. The Sacrifice would not see the SUNSET.

35

Mo Journal Entry 14

THE FOUR OF us, armed to the literal teeth made our way to the rear fire exit. Easy watched our collective back as we plodded down the hall. We could occasionally catch wind of prison employees racing to or from the stairs. Thankfully, no one came in a fire exit and we ran into no one during our trek. We had so many guns that we probably couldn't have raised one even if needed. The explosions from above began right as we left the armory. Following the third boom, I was hoping to see our fellow escapees come to meet us, their plans going off without a hitch.

We rested next to the red door. Smokes offered between gulps of air, "Jumpsuit's da Sacrifice, yo." Before I could ask what he meant, the couple of demolitionists burst through the stairwell door. Tychus was using The Expert as a crutch.

Motherfucker! Do we have to have one of these in every damn journal? If I thought I could spare the effort, I would've thrown something at The Oracle. He knew! The fat bastard could've just fucking told us and this old dude would've made it out, but now he's probably going to die! We could try to carry him, but that would just slow all of us down and get more of us killed. Shit, there's probably some other reason he needed to stay behind anyway, undoubtedly making sure the rest of us would make it. I hate the logic of this screenplay.

I sucked in through my teeth. "How bad is it?"

Hammer opened her mouth to respond, but The Loner beat her to it. He shakily offered, "Shattered fibula. I expected a lot more blood and pain but Hammer dumped some sulfa powder on it. It mostly just aches now. I'm not going with you, I will only slow you down. I'll go to the roof and keep them busy with a rifle."

I hate to say it, but I'd known this was coming.

I've got to ask: sulfa powder? What the fuck is this, Saving Private Ryan? I had no idea where you would find that stuff or that it was even produced in the 21st-century. She must keep her sulfa powder stored right beside her eight tracks and her crocheting kit inside of her Model T, or wherever she was hiding supplies.

Zombies On A Plane

He gestured to a bagged rifle my brother had leaned against the wall. "What's in there?"

It was apparent through the cloth casing that the rifle was equipped with a scope. Easy unzipped it and began, "It's a–" The injured janitor picked up, "A scoped M 14. That's my girl! I got the marksmanship award for shooting mine."

My brother ensured the magazine was loaded before handing over the dealer of death. I was bursting at the seams to say the soldiers prayer. Tychus looked to the expert beside him as he used the covered sniper rifle as a crutch to back away. "I can take care of the guys in the towers and keep them off your backs. Get away from here and I will be happy."

Before he could turn, The Oracle reached out and gave him a couple of pistols. "Fo close quatas, cuz."

Well fuck, I'll just be a worthless piece of shit sandwiched between two competent, forward thinking tacticians, my perfect brother and my hefty friend. I feel useless when everyone around me does something of use and I just stand here like a mute idiot.

The Expert almost broke as she ordered him. She commanded, "Stay alive soldier. We'll come back for you when the coast is clear!"

Before disappearing, The Sacrifice smiled. "You know where I'll be," and just like that, he was gone.

Damn. I had been hoping to take him back to the island. The Tech would be jealous that I found someone with such an awesome name. It was nearly as cool as finding a survivor named Jean-Luc or Gandalf. I said "nearly as cool," either of those would be nerdgasmic! Of course, my rude ass didn't wish him luck or even say goodbye, surely adding "inept asshole" to Aka's friendly descriptors of me.

I was just thinking, where's his cat? I thought that it had been with him when we left this morning. I need to ask The Oracle if Adjutant had played the role of The Innocent.

Hammer interrupted my thoughts with a laugh, "You know, y'all didn't have to bring the entire armory with you. We can't carry all this."

I was going to remind her that if we had not, Tychus wouldn't have found the perfect sniper rifle and we would all die horribly. But I was still catching my breath, exhausted from carrying three times my body weight.

Zombies On A Plane

Smokes's "you's always at da place you is always post to be" flashed across my mind. I agree, everything happens for a reason. Shit, it's creepy to be around an actual prophet; I'm just glad he's on our side.

I leaned on something that looked like an MP5, M4, or possibly a UB40. "Well just grab what you want and let's go."

The earlier explosions had sent alarms blaring and my brother's fiancée's logical deduction could barely be heard. She spoke like we were in a library, "Yeah, but we shouldn't start our escape until we start hearing gunfire from the roof or at least make sure no one is watching. We can open the door though, I think we've set off every alarm in this building."

Uncharacteristically, Smokes took some initiative. He moved to prop the door open with a rifle.

Hammer waited halfway out the door, listening for a sharpshooter as the radio in my vest chimed. I looked down and was confused; my father and I had discussed that we would wait for our nightly chats as to not interrupt the other at an inopportune time. I cut my eyes at Smokes who widened his. He nodded, expecting this.

Unsure if I had really heard anything, I looked down at the radio as if it were going to tell me why it had buzzed. I questioned into the radio, "Hello?"

Daddy came back, "Mo, Gray Fox here, wasn't sure if you could talk. How's the escape going? Over."

"We had to," I paused, "make some alterations. We're about to start our run. I'll get back with you in a few minutes." I didn't add, "Or we'll all be dead. You'll figure it out."

My dad spoke calmly, "Sounds like y'all will all make it back." I heard rapid gunfire in the background from over the radio. "But we are under attack right now. Y'all should probably hold off on showing up until after we deal with this. Over."

I gave The Oracle a pleading stare as I replied, "What? By who? Why?"

We could've played twenty questions, but he replied, "Not sure, they appear to have military equipment and–" his transmission was abruptly ended with sudden static following what sounded like the report of a rifle. The Oracle simultaneously shouted at my side in a singsong voice, "To the left, to the left."

Zombies On A Plane

He pushed me to the side with both hands as the radio dissolved into static. Did he really just do The Heisman on that Mo? I probably would have gotten into a heated argument with him in which I would wind up being the militia member that dragged black people behind his truck. I surprised myself by completely ignoring that Smokes had just pushed me to the ground for no reason. Maybe I was more shocked at hearing my father apparently killed over the radio. Does that mean I'm not completely self-centered?

I looked between all of my compatriots as The Oracle gestured to the door. "We gots to get, mufuckas!"

No shit, dumbass. At that very moment, the captain alerted us it was time to begin our final march. We moved as one to the door. This was it, we'd either be cut in half before we made it to the plane or the Collins family would have a full reunion, provided, of course that my parents weren't already dead. Actually, we could also make it to *Alex* and then Smokes could crash us into an open field; optimism comes naturally to ME.

Javan Bonds

36

Mo Journal Entry 15

HAMMER STUCK HER head around the corner of the building, raised and kept her rifle on an enemy until he ran past without noticing our crew. We followed her around the corner and I silently thanked God that all of the building's windows were too high for anyone to see directly down into the yard. We saw no movement in the towers as we came to the front corner. There was no sound, other than the distant fieldworkers; we assumed our sniper was keeping silent over-watch. All of the cellblocks and other buildings were on the opposite side of this main complex. Only the exercise yard stood between us and the double fence. It was empty, naturally. Inmates wouldn't be involved in recreational activities when they could work the fields.

The Expert pointed in the general direction of the trees and the lake beyond. I had to ask, "Really? I'd rather not be in the woods with the peevies. We can't stay on the road?"

"We will follow the creek back to the lake. If you see any Ruskies, get in the water."

That was fairly logical. I made no retort as we walked past some basketball hoops. She tossed a grenade at the first fence, waiting for it to separate cleanly. The captain repeated the process with the outer fence. Just as our group came to the hole in the first fence, I heard the faint wailing of an alarm begin. There was no need to worry about that, it would pose no problem once we were in the woods, or so I hoped. We moved into the open area and we were free. What a boring escape! I hadn't even been fired upon directly and there hasn't been enough violence. Should I make something up here? Jesus, why you gotta give me such a hard time? I'm trying to write an end-of-days journal; I need to fear for my life!

The sun was shining down on us and there wasn't a cloud in the sky, yadda, yadda. I was about to mention something of the anti-climactic-ness of our escape and how we had made it almost cartoonishly unscathed. Before I could open my mouth, a fat, blue naked man stepped out into the light. His face was covered in blood and gore; he was chowing down on an unidentifiable piece of sloppy meat. Man, I need to learn to shut the fuck up, careful what you wish for and all that, not even *think* things are going easy. The entire group stopped to stare at it.

Zombies On A Plane

The monster nonchalantly went to town on its bounty with gusto. The blue cannibal realized it had an audience and stopped to look at us in kind.

My first thought after seeing this creature was: "Santa Claus?" Even through the grotesque, bloody meat, it was obvious that the zombie's beard and hair were white. This monster made Smokes look like a successful Jenny Craig customer and I noticed a thin coat of white fuzz all over its body. Is this something common? I have not seen this on the younger infected and I have not personally been close enough to an older adult to inspect its body hair. You know, I don't like the prospect of being mauled and all of that. It would probably make this movie closer to PG if this thing's sheet of hair had been just a little bit thicker below the waist. Of course upon thinking that, I had to look down at Jolly old St. Peevie's shriveled junk. Imagine a midget nudist living in Antarctica and you would have a close approximation to what hung before me. I would never again want anything for Christmas besides a mind wash.

Other than it appeared the Blue Man Crew had just recruited a really fat senior citizen, the most noticeable aspect of Peevie Claus was his eyes: they weren't a single yellow orb.

Sure, the whites of the eyes still had a yellow tint to them, but unlike every undead I had seen since the beginning of armageddon, the pupils were visible and extra creepy. The pupils were a sickly yellow, the color of a healing bruise. The rest of the eye had the same neon flash as any other infected.

I gazed up at the blazing sun with stupid amazement. The creature lifted its head from a dismembered morsel to follow my eyes.

When it realized it was standing in direct sunlight, it dropped its stare back to us, cocked its head like a confused dog, screamed before dropping its meal and rushed at us. "What the–" my question was interrupted by the boom of Smokes's shotgun. "Sko sko sko mufuckas!" We ran forward past the headless blue Santa-corpse, blood spraying into a pool where the cranium would normally be. Our "run" just became literally a fucking run.

Are you shitting me? Was that just a one-time thing or can they all come out in the daytime now? Why the hell would they wait until this moment to discover sunlight was cool? We could have broken out of prison yesterday and at least then we would only have had to deal with human antagonists.

Zombies On A Plane

My entire party began mowing down attacking peevies. I questioned the Oracle between shots. "What–the–fuck?"

"Thangs change, cuz."

Yeah, but why? I had so many questions. This shit was like one of those video games that was impossible to beat. There were just no extra lives or cheat codes. God, I miss the Internet sometimes.

Our true antagonists were everywhere. The evil humans had been nothing more than a slight diversion from the main plot. We were dropping ravenous zombies like flies, blue piles of shit covered, bloody, shrunken testicles surrounded us, moaning, angry, reaching for our yummy flesh. The Expert obviously carried endless supplies of ammo and was holding them back effectively. Maybe she has some of those cheat codes; perhaps she can spare a wall hack. All of us still remained a step away from the water; I managed not to drown myself in the rush.

After what seemed like hours, we could see the lake open before us. There were dozens of cannibal nudists between us and safety. We began to move on alongside the shore and in the direction of *Alex*.

This meant we only had to cover three directions. Why didn't we just fucking swim, you ask? Well, for one thing I'm about as good at treading water as Gene. Plus, knowing my luck, the peevies would also spontaneously become Michael Phelps!

We pushed ourselves inside the plane and I shuddered. "I think I have seen more penis today than any time in my entire life." Aka glared at me with disgust, horrified that I used such language. As if I was the only one that noticed all of the nasty blue genitals bum-rushing us.

Just as she turned away, she gasped and flung herself back. A blue twig and a set of blueberries suddenly hit and plastered themselves against the outside of the window right at her face. The cannibal nudists were lunging at the plane and trying to get in. Our painful deaths were nearly guaranteed.

I was looking outside, wondering if we could take off with peevies (not pigs) climbing on the wing. Smokes was at my side but it could easily have been Samuel L Jackson. "Get these motherfucking zombies off my motherfucking plane!"

Zombies On A Plane

I had to bite my tongue to keep from laughing. I really don't know why I pick these fucking inopportune moments to see humor in things, but that was the perfect parody of a movie quote for the situation at hand. I shouted, "Everybody get to this side of the plane!"

Somehow the small aircraft did not tip as my over weighty friend hefted his bulk against me. I would compare it to cradling a baby Godzilla. I wonder if his mother had to deal with this when he was a baby. It seemed to work as the peevies followed us on around the outside of the windows. The Expert was thinking on my wavelength again; she rushed to the other side and threw open the door. The Expert was watching and waiting for the undead to try and take advantage of this new opening. She sat there with a pistol in each hand, blowing each monster into the water as it came into her sites. With the right wing almost touching the water, the exploded gray matter and warm blood from the recently shot peevies poured down onto our disgusted huddle. Fortunately, the bulk of The Oracle basically shielded my entire body, so I was spared the majority of gore raining down on me. His left side was drenched in the offal of former humans. I promised myself I would not mention this to him; I really didn't want to break his fragile resolve while he was controlling a plane we were in.

For one thing, I didn't think it was possible to fire dual pistols simultaneously, but I guess she proved *MythBusters* and physics wrong. I think I was the only other person in the plane that was hearing the theme song to Halo. Also, try to imagine being inside the drum set at a Def Leppard concert and you will have a pretty good idea of the stress that unloading two XD pistols in the cabin of a small plane puts on your eardrums. I was surprised not to see blood running out of anyone's ears.

Captain Sledge smiled, satisfied she had eliminated the tangos and caused irreparable damage to our cochlear nerves. As if she thought we were able to hear, she slammed the door before taking a seat in the back and began speaking. "Let's get this show on the road!"

Smokes thankfully got out of my lap and it was amazing I did not have any broken bones or ruptured organs. The Oracle started the ignition, picking up speed as I waved goodbye to what looked like a Chippendale's Chris Farley. We began lifting off as the herd of insane naked people tried to chase us from the shore.

I already knew the truth, but The Oracle flew over the prison grounds so the others could see The Sacrifice. The Loner's body lay in a pile of spent casings and a pool of his own blood, playing his final scene.

Zombies On A Plane

He had obviously done his job or we would probably be dead from gunshots. It's kinda depressing to realize that we are only alive now because of the roles assigned to us. Is that what they call survivor's guilt?

I tried to shake off the unsettling mix of doubt and understanding. The Oracle steered us in the direction of Guntersville to save the city. Maybe we would make it in time to save my mother and The Love Interest. It was too late for my father, but maybe I would definitely wreak some VENGEANCE.

Javan Bonds

37

The Breakout

JOHN POINTED DOWN to his left. "What are those people doing?"

Herb and John were sitting in the guard tower, expecting another easy day like usual. When John pointed to the group, Herb lifted his sniper rifle and scoped in on the people moving in the direction of the fence. After entirely too long of his staring at the black girl's ass, John grunted. "Well?"

"Oh. They have guns."

"Who the hell are they and why do they have guns?"

Herb continued to keep an eye on the group, they seem to move with some kind of intent. John used his walkie-talkie to call up the Warden and ascertain why there were apparent civilians walking around with firearms.

"The boss ain't answering; just keep watching 'em."

He tried the other tower; they had no idea who those people were. John reached for the bullhorn to call out to the armed people down below and Herb kept his aim on the redhead in front.

He raised the horn to begin yelling as the woman in front lifted something small out of her pocket. Herb asked, "A grenade?"

She tossed what looked like a baseball to the fence and three seconds later it exploded. The guards drew back in surprise; seconds passed before Herb thought to pull up the rifle, ready to fire.

The woman drew another grenade and immediately tossed it at the second fence. The smoke had not even settled from the first explosion, she seemed in a hurry. "Fuck me!" John reached over to press the button that would sound the perimeter alarm.

His partner was a millisecond away from pulling the trigger and stopping these maniacs as a projectile sunk into one side of his neck and exploded out the other.

John was bathed in his partner's blood, and was so shocked by the gory death beside him, he froze.

It took him a second to realize what just happened before he slammed his hand down on the remote for the klaxon.

Not thinking about where the bullet that just destroyed his friend had come from, he picked up the dropped rifle and began sighting in on the runners below. Before he got his aim, his brains were splattered on the desk beside him.

The north guard tower was in disarray. They heard a couple of shots but had no clue of the escapees on the far side of the other tower. Greg and Mike were playing cards, taken by surprise when shots were fired and sirens started blaring.

Mike yelled to be heard and pointed to the administration building. Once he realized there was a shooter on the roof, he quickly lowered to the floor as he spoke. "Shooter on top of main building!"

Greg similarly lowered and pulled back the action to his sniper rifle. "I saw him! What the fuck is going on?"

Mike started switching through the short band channels and could tell from the frantic screaming over the radio that the other employees were just as clueless. "Hell if I know! That fucker must have shot John and that other guy!"

Greg had already assumed this and was planning to take out the gunman. He aimed at the general location of the sniper and quickly rose over the barrier to take the shot.

Tychus hit the ground, keeping his eye fixed on the guard with the rifle . He had taken out the other tower before either of the guards knew what was going on, but he was sure these two had been paying more attention. The old janitor knew he wasn't going to make it off these grounds, but he was confident that the others had been given enough time to break through the fences. The wailing of the alarms steeled his resolve.

Zombies On A Plane

Greg raised up from the floor cautiously, gun at the ready, planning to blow this lone gunman away. He shot up from his hiding place, his scope came into focus; he could see only the briefest darkening through the zoomed reticle.

The Sacrifice watched the guard launch himself upright. Thankfully, he had not changed positions before exposing himself again and the stupid prison guard simply popped back into the crosshairs like a shooting gallery target.

Greg collapsed before he could get a shot off, killed instantly as the heavy caliber round crashed through his skull. His lifeless corpse faced Mike, the rifle with the destroyed scope flung to his other side. Mike could see a clean hole where his eye used to be; light from the hole at the back of his ruptured cranium streamed through the empty socket just before it began filling with blood. There was no way in hell he was going to try to take a shot at this marksman and decided the best course would be to crawl downstairs and hide until this was over.

Tychus knew the hostile remaining in the tower had retreated after a few seconds of watching nothing; it was that kind of delay. He would attempt to remain vigilant just in case someone took a shot at him from the tower, but he now felt safe to focus on the door leading to the roof. Now that they knew someone was up here, they would surely be coming with guns blazing.

Two prison employees threw themselves out of the stairwell door without even looking first; all Tychus had to do was squeeze the trigger and his targets fell with ease, peppered with holes. The next assaulters were much slower and careful, opening the door first then ducking away. A shaking hand holding a pistol raised into his vision and The Sacrifice severed it with a 762. Screams from both men echoed in the hallway as the stump pulled back down and grew fainter as the new amputee and his partner ran for cover.

His attackers were getting smarter; they tossed a smoke grenade to land in front of the door. With his loaded pistols and half a dozen magazines of rifle ammo, Tychus wasn't afraid to send rounds at random intervals into the smoke. Hundreds of shell casings lay around him; no one had dared to fire back. On his second to last M14 mag, a voice called through the smoke. A shaken man asked, "What do you want?"

Zombies On A Plane

They must have thought he was a disgruntled prisoner. He smiled and offered, "I just wanted to keep you busy."

This was Tychus's final stand and he knew it, but damn if it wasn't a blaze of glory. He had been a quiet, solitary janitor since leaving active duty all those years ago; as long as Hammer and the others made it home, his death would mean something. He smiled. He was going to give them all the time he could. "If you let me go, I'll throw down my rifle and come out with hands up." The Loner detested lying, but had to extend the game as long as possible.

"You can go wherever you want."

The janitor audibly threw down his rifle and armed men began slowly walking through the smoke. One of them already had cuffs unclipped to detain him, he simply waited for them to get closer.

There were three men less than a handful of feet from him and he pulled both pistols from his waistband. They could take him, but they wouldn't take him ALIVE.

Javan Bonds

38

Still The Villain

"Fine, you can go."

Sally squealed as she made her way into the lead Humvee. Bobbitt was confident she would not come to harm in an armed and armored convoy made up of their Humvee, an LATV, and three heavy personnel carriers. He didn't want to argue with his only source of pussy, plus he just wanted to get a move on. The lead villain knew how much Sally despised her former overlords and neighbors; it couldn't hurt to give her a front row seat to their invasion of the island. He decided this is what Marines had felt as they anticipated attacking Iwo Jima. The Captain could nearly picture a squadron of his men raising the Stars & Stripes over the corpses of these traitors.

He was hoping to have found more armor over the past few weeks, something even heavier than their 40mm grenade launcher and chain guns.

The Bradley tank that he had been forced to abandon in Douglas had disappeared–fucking hillbillies had probably taken it apart piece by piece and used it to make a moonshine still. This whole endeavor would have been less difficult if his mish-mashed company had stumbled upon an M1 Abrams. Bobbitt silently cursed himself for not sending some men to scout Fort McClellan in Anniston. Oh well, these inbreeds surely won't stand a chance with their plastic Storm Trooper armor and a few bolt action rifles versus the chain fed mini-guns of the federal government. America would again be victorious over these stupid secessionists!

Before the faintest hint of dawn started to crest the horizon, The Villain readied himself for glorious battle. Bobbitt, Sally, thirty-two infantrymen, and a four-man SOF crew chugged away in their convoy of an LATV, Bobbitt's personal Humvee, and three massive MRAPs to capture enemy territory.

The line of armored vehicles came to a stop on the highway at the top of the mountain. The sniper team climbed out of the LATV, the two soldiers accompanying Bobbitt in his Humvee replaced them in their vehicle. The marksman team headed off to find a good vantage point from which to snipe as all five vehicles again began moving forward.

Zombies On A Plane

The Captain was confused to see the jet-ski and pontoon moved away from the gap between the bridge and the causeway at the bottom of the mountain. He had thought Earl had earlier left it connected, but The Villain could see the gap had been un-bridged.

He could also see a pair of desert camouflaged Humvees barricading the causeway on the other side of the small guardhouse.

He quickly grabbed Sally's shoulder and nearly threw her to the floor, he knew what this was. The captain shouted, "Get down!" He swerved to his left, driving behind a shopping center and a parking lot full of cars. As soon as he began to change direction, a couple of pockmarked spider webs appeared on the windshield.

"One Humvee, a similar vehicle, at least three MRAPs following. All broke off eastward between Days Inn and the gas bank. Rajesh was not able to terminate the Humvee driver. Over." One of The Phantoms–Randy was positive it was Kumar–gave a brief report to the general audience and over the radio to their fifth Indian comrade.

The assault had begun.

The mayor whistled. "MRAPs are mean sumbitches. Did you see the mounts?" Mine Resistant Ambush Protected vehicles (a.k.a. US Military Cougars) were heavily armored monsters that could easily brush off 50 cal rounds and were impervious to almost everything besides rocket launchers. They were being faced with some heavy machinery. Randy wished now he had taken the time to learn how to operate the Bradley when Hammer was around.

Kumar lowered his binoculars. "At least one 40mm grenade launcher."

Mayor Collins dropped his chin and began lifting his radio. "I think we might need to call for reinforcements."

The convoy came to a halt when Bobbitt felt they had reached moderate safety. He knew that with more than one Humvee and possibly access to Earl's radio, the insurgents were bound to be listening. Eavesdropping? The captain needed to communicate with his men but too exposed outside. And yet he said, "Earl has obviously been compromised, we've been expected. It's time to give them what they've been waiting for!"

Zombies On A Plane

Bobbitt assumed Earl was dead; at least he knew the spy would wish for death rather than face the enraged captain. The military convoy circled the gas bank, well out of the line of sight of their enemy. The convoy stopped in the Top O' the River parking lot to dispense eight grunts from each Cougar. These boots on the ground would dish out havoc from all directions. The mounted guns would ruin the enemy's shit. Bobbitt hoped all these distractions would lead to the defeat of the INSURGENTS.

Javan Bonds

39

Designated Targets

SALLY WAS OVERWHELMED with joy. She could only imagine how great it was going to be to watch these deranged libertarians suffer at the hands of her federal benefactors. They stopped at some grimy old restaurant and the trucks of soldiers unloaded. The men had been instructed to stay in well lit areas while peppering the island with small arms fire. All of them carried a rifle, pistols, and most had several grenades.

The secondary betrayer was glad they did not make her tote one of those devices of death. Sally Dick had been told a gun could just randomly fire like it was actually malicious. Guns *did* kill people and they should only be used by the military or by policemen–people who were professionals trained by professionals. That Hammer lady that had been the sheriff had been in the military and a couple of the police on the island were real cops from before, so she didn't mind their carrying weapons.

Even if most of the survivors on the island were stupid rednecks clinging to their guns and religion, firearms were dangerous and you needed training to operate them. What really pissed her off was that damn Mayor with a fucking hand cannon on his hip that thought everyone had a right to bear arms. Fucking constitutionalists. The former social worker couldn't wait to see this bastard get what he deserved–a bullet from the people that give out the privilege of rights.

The call for more defenders was answered by the majority of island dwellers who showed up with basic civilian armaments. Their home was under direct attack and they were not going to go gently into the night. The Phantom squad's long-range marksman, Dr. Philip George, was among several defenders in or surrounding the Best Western. He was using a 308 backing up the islanders who had hunting rifles of various calibers. The Medicine Man rested the barrel of his rifle on the lip of an upper story window when he heard the motor of an MRAP rev. The vehicle came to rest squarely facing the causeway and the defenders behind the barricades. It opened fire and decimated the Humvees, striking several of those who had just answered the call for reinforcements.

Zombies On A Plane

Some plunged into the water to avoid being minced, others sent rounds harmlessly back at the cougar. His Indian brothers and the mayor used the engine blocks of the never-to-run-again vehicles and the reinforced wall of the guardhouse as cover; dozens of shots pinged uselessly off the armor. It only took a split second for the doctor to sight in and fire into the barrel of the cougar's mounted weapon. This clearly would not injure the gunner; the doctor was just happy to have turned the cougar into nothing more than a defenseless APC.

Mayor Collins accompanied the commandos onto the gravel bank on the western side of the causeway. They hustled back to the island with no assaulting rounds from behind. Carnage surrounded them; the barrage had been unleashed for only seconds but was nonetheless devastating.

The SOF sharpshooters were in position and had direct line of sight all the way to Publix at the hotel across the highway. Rather than take out the several visible targets and risk compromising their location, the team chose to wait and lineup on the civilian closest to the enemy commandos; a man talking on a walkie-talkie who carried himself as a person in command.

The sniper had his 50 lined up just above the man's sternum and fired.

Dr. George scanned the opposite side of the lake, looking for targets beyond the occasional foot soldier. He caught a flash in the far distance, near his 2 o'clock. The Phantom cardiologist knew before he heard the heavy crack of the large round that the opposition had brought their own long-range snipers. He raised his rifle to pinpoint where he had seen the flash and finally found the shooter perched on an outcropping of the mountain. He had no clue what the enemy sniper had just targeted or if the target had been hit. The Medicine Man nearly smiled as he knew it would be this particular enemy's last shot.

Dropping back down from the recoil after his initial shot, Sgt. Huggins peered out and was more than surprised to see nothing where his decimated target should now be laying. There was no eviscerated body, no blood, absolutely nothing. He almost asked his spotter how the fuck that happened. The Sergeant heard a single shot from far away.

"Did you see–" was all the SOF shooter got out before his brain exploded through the back of his skull. Bone fragments and what looked like gray and bloody scrambled eggs littered the ground behind his body.

Zombies On A Plane

Below, Captain Jonathan Bobbitt rested safely behind his Humvee as he strategized with his commanding soldiers. He forced Sally into the open MRAP to keep her protected and from interrupting sensitive plans. She would have liked to see more of the stupid yokels slaughtered under the mighty fist of the US military, but she was content to remain safe.

Bobbitt looked up through the thin covering trees as the men around him discussed where the grenade launcher would be of the greatest use. "The troops could begin massing to the east while a heavy machine gun cougar strafed back and forth across 431, harassing–" The commander was interrupted by an echoing shot from the enemy. The leader of The Villains could see the muzzle flash of a lone sniper from a top floor window in the hotel and pointed. "Cougar, send some grenades into the top floor of the hotel!"

The gunner of the MRAP launched a steady barrage of rocket propelled explosives at the area where Bobbitt pointed. Whoever the sniper was, he would never take another shot at THEM.

Javan Bonds

40

Flanked

THE SOF TEAM had just radioed that they'd lost their sniper. Bobbitt was guessing he had seen the kill shot from the enemy's only military trained long-range sniper. That problem had just been removed…permanently.

One cougar still made its harassing strafing runs past the causeway. The Captain ordered the driver to halt in an open position and was delighted to see that the sniper who had damaged the other cougar was silent. The subordinate commanders rushed into the grenade launching APC. Sally hurriedly rushed out as the vehicle moved to launch some heavy rounds across the causeway.

"–I ain't got no idea. I guess I just tripped. It was almost like somebody shoved me down, but nobody was that close."

One of The Phantoms listened to the unexplainable miracle that had just saved the mayor's life. "It is a good thing whatever it was happened when it did. A sniper bullet destroyed your radio as you fell."

This had to be divine intervention. Randy looked up, thankful to The Screenwriter, where ever he was.

Captain Bobbitt opened the Humvee driver's door and Sally began walking around the front to the opposite side. From behind him, he heard the slap of bare skin on asphalt. The Villain slowly turned around, confused as to why a soldier had taken his boots off. What the fuck? It wasn't a soldier at all, it was a dirty and naked child walking casually through the sunlight. This child had something of a blue tint to its skin; it looked at the captain calmly with its animal-like, yellow eyes. Bobbitt could see the LATV parked and empty only steps away. It was a higher lift and the mounted gun was enclosed. It would be safer than this tin can on wheels. He realized he and his concubine needed to have a plan quick if the zombies were suddenly tolerant of sunlight.

Zombies On A Plane

His girlfriend froze upon hearing the sound as well. He spoke to her calmly without taking his eyes from the peevie. "Sally, get into the LATV. Slowly."

The captain slowly lifted his pistol from its leg holster as they both began creeping to the truck. The infected cannibal turned, tracking their movement. It was clear this small monster felt no ill effects from the sunlight. It let out a monstrous howl that Bobbitt wouldn't have thought could come from such a small former-human. Suddenly the blue child charged.

The thing dropped after five rounds but its forward momentum slid the carcass almost to Bobbitt's feet. He turned and ran, pushing Sally along. "Go, go, fucking go!"

They secured themselves in the LATV. "Why was that thing out in the daylight, Jonathan?"

The Villain began to lift his radio as he responded, "Fuck if I know! Can they all do that now?"

Sally shrugged as he made a call over the radio. "Cougars: this is Bobbitt coming to you from the LATV. We just had an infected charge us in the daylight. Be ready for anything. And the zombies are the new priority for the MRAPs."

"Yeah," the mayor joked. "Sure would suck to be on the other side of the water." Dr. George had told them of this development in the infected. He had radioed that the enemy combatants would likely be attacked by the infected before he sedated the captured peevie and came to join the fight himself. Mayor Collins pointed up to the top story of the Best Western. "Who you think was up there?"

All of the defenders had tactically withdrawn to at least the distance of Bottom Dollar. That cougar was spitting out grenades like it had an infinite supply. Randy nearly chuckled, his oldest son would probably accuse them of using cheat codes.

They were now on the far side of the building and could no longer see the destroyed window. Kumar knew where he was pointing and grew somber. "I think it was our sniper." They were all thinking about the only professionally trained long-range shooter defending the island. Aware of Philip George's marksmanship, the mayor swelled with pride. "Well, maybe he took a few of them bastards out first!"

The Phantoms felt like sadly cheering. They hoped their squad mate had dropped some of the military lunatics. It was at least an honorable death.

Zombies On A Plane

The military vehicles started receiving dozens of radio calls. Literally all of the soldiers on foot were desperately running away from the naked monsters. Sporadic gunfire could be heard over the radios. This catastrophic symphony was mixed with bursts from the LATV and heavy machine gun of the MRAP mowing down occasional peevies. All the while, the 40mm pounded grenades across the causeway. The soldiers were on their way and they needed cover or they were just going to break into the armor.

"I need one man from the cougar to drive the MRAP with the disabled gun and pick up the troops," Bobbitt called over his radio, "and don't waste time or I'll just call out a name at random."

The back door of the rocket launching cougar flew open and a man walked out. He stopped to either wave or flip off the Captain. Just as he did this, something hard hit the ground at his feet and bounced into the crew compartment of the MRAP.

Javan Bonds

41

Mo Journal Entry 16

AFTER TAKEOFF AND the removal of our attempted stowaways, the journey home was relatively silent. Smokes almost deserves congratulations for not incessantly jabbering. I wrote in my journal to keep myself occupied. Hammer repeatedly checked that every weapon was locked and loaded. Aka watched out the window like she had not flown across the fucking ocean to get to this country. Easy was probably thinking about steroids or muscle milk or protein bars or tanning lotion. Actually, I knew my brother was just as worried about our father as I was. His fiancée had to be worried about her future father-in-law. And The Expert was simply trying not to think about her secret, straight-crush being killed. I imagine Smokes was picturing chocolate covered sugar butter or something equally unhealthy.

We reached familiar landmarks and were nearly to Albertville and we all knew we would soon be at death's doorstep. Easy questioned, "We can roll these windows down, right?"

"Mufuckin' white people," the prophet sighed. "DIS ain't no git-er-dun 4x4! We in a advanced piece a machinery–"

I cut in with a laugh. "But you can't lower the windows? Yeah, advanced."

My rotund friend glared daggers at me. Our own Kathy Bates impersonator spoke up, "I think there are MRAPs in that group of enemy vehicles." She paused and squinted her eye before continuing, "One of them is opening its backdoor! Roll down the window!"

Smokes was incredulous. "Lady, was you not just fuckin' in here when I told that other cracka–" he was cut off by the explosion of a pistol. Hammer had just shot out the small window on his door.

I saw The Oracle's mouth move and knew it had to be another one of his strange exclamations. Something about "colic nuggets."

Zombies On A Plane

I could not hear myself talk after another explosion. "Was that really fucking necessary Cap? You could have given the pilot a heart attack!"

I think we're all going to have long-term hearing problems anyway, but I don't think she had to add to it. Somehow Smokes was able to remain conscious and even kept the plane steady with a bullet traveling just past his head.

We were lined up with the highway and would soon be on top of the enemy. The Expert dropped a live frag out of the permanently rolled down window just as we flew over the opened APC.

The grenade bounced neatly into the vehicle and exploded, nothing more than a puff out the back. I stared blankly at Hammer after seeing the excitement of nothing more than a smoke grenade going off. She shouted over the roar of the engine and the wind, "What? I wasn't expecting fireworks. Just taking care of the occupants." She then added to make it sound even better, "Oh, and it didn't mess up the guts, so we'll be able to use that vehicle after."

Yeah, but I don't want to be the first person to go in there. I'm the only one that laughed at her mention of guts. Smokes had brought us to a ridiculously low altitude and speed for Hammer to pull that off.

That had to be it, this wasn't *really* a movie. Before I was able to make a comment on the new paint job on the inside of that APC, the little truck beside the now silent rocket launcher sent a spray of machine gun bullets up at *Alex*.

After a few snaps and smoke pouring from the engine, I looked at my compatriots expecting to see someone dead or dying. I shouted, "Anyone's ass bleeding!?" All passengers and the pilot responded in the negative. Every one of us remained miraculously not dead yet.

Smokes fought the controls for a few seconds, but eventually began bringing the plane down over the water on its final descent. Wow, the three of us actually made it home with our intended goal on board. I am still surprised The Oracle did not plow us into the ground on the outbound or return trip. This plane may never fly again but it did more than I expected; it kept me from dying an excruciatingly horrible death. If I'm able to survive the swim from the plane to land without getting Ebola or some kind of super AIDS from the open sewer that is now the lake.

Zombies On A Plane

I'm going to have to see about turning *Alex* into a memorial. Wouldn't that be cool? It could be some kind of statue of a single engine plane with water skis. In generations, people can take their kids to it to learn about a dude named after a comedienne who flew hundreds of miles to save his brother. Of course then the brother would become the main character of the story and it would focus on how everything he did was great and how he saved the world.

Smokes was able to bring her down on the south side of the eastern causeway. We landed close enough to the island to be out of sight of the enemy jeeps and maybe near enough that with a long jump we wouldn't even have to fully immerse ourselves in raw sewage.

Man, it's good to be HOME.

Javan Bonds

42

Mo Journal Entry 17

SHE HAD OPENED the door and The Expert was preparing to launch herself to the shore. We distinctly heard a small motorboat approaching. The five of us waited–okay, I cowered in the floorboard for what seemed like hours while everybody else waited and watched with rifles at the ready. A machine gun mounted bass boat came from around the pontoon bridge at the opened gap. I peeked over the lip of the window after Smokes said something about "Dat Star Trek mufucka." I was happy to see that it was the tech, wearing Brotherhood of Steel power armor with the helmet by his side. Of course he was wearing his customary adamantium claws rather than the suit's gauntlets. He proudly steered the PT boat christened: "Moldy Crow."

I smiled and shook my head as I waved. "Hey Kyle Katarn!"

He looked over with surprise; yeah, smoking planes do not crash into the lake every day. Actually, maybe he was just surprised that we were alive, not engulfed in a massive fireball. The Tech also seemed genuinely glad to see us.

"Mo!" He scrunched up his face in a poor impersonation of Yoda, "Strong with you the Force must be." He dropped out of his geekier than usual stance and asked, "Can I help?"

The boat drifted to within feet of the Beaver as I pointed over my shoulder at my brother and Aka. I then looked at my other two partners who readily agreed. "You need to take these two to the island. The three of us can go with you."

He nodded before ordering his Spartan gunner, "Take these civilians to the courthouse and the other three will stay with me. Looks like you get the day off, John." I seriously doubt the man wearing green Halo armor was actually named John, but The Tech gave a nerdy grin when he uttered the name. He and I were the only two of the assembled group that would know John is the name of the Master Chief. Hell, nobody else even knew he was wearing Mjolnir armor. God, I'm a fucking nerd; at least Gene knew what I was thinking as he sent Easy off to see our mother.I don't know if it's just what I wanted to hear, but I was elated when the armored soldier saluted and sounded exactly like a Storm Trooper. "Yes sir!" Damn, now that I think about it, I should've thanked the guy who had been on the 50 for not turning us into Swiss cheese when I screamed and waved like an imbecile.

Amazingly, the hefty pilot had not sunk our tiny, leaking craft. Even as he stepped from the plane to the boat, neither tipped over. I asked the tech after we dropped off the passengers, "So what's been going on?"

"You mean you don't know?"

Yeah, I knew we'd just bombed an APC, but I still had no clue to the big picture. "Well, I know we're being attacked, but that's about it." I figured the fact that our plane had been riddled with bullets would have given him some indication that we were aware of hostiles.

I could see Gene mentally preparing for several parsecs worth of story. "I guess I gotta start just after you LEFT…"

Javan Bonds

43

Gonads

THE TWO NEWCOMERS followed the armored man before them at a brisk pace. The helmeted soldier sounded a bit like those guys from Star Wars when he turned his helmeted head in Easy's direction. "So who are you?"

He gestured to his fiancée as he spoke. "I'm Easy, Mo's brother. This is my fiancée, Aka."

He could almost see the eyebrows raise through the faceplate. "Oh! I guess that means we're going to see your mom."

The Protector nodded as he realized he was soon to see his mother but would never again see his father alive. Since they had crash landed in the water, everything had happened so fast that he'd had no time to ask or even think about the fate of his dad.

The trio rounded the corner to Gunter. Easy had to stop and blink. A woman that appeared to be his mother was walking in their direction, a young woman beside her. Both were wearing what appeared to be Kevlar with assault rifles strapped over each shoulder. "Mama?"

She broke from her conversation with the other woman and froze similarly before shouting and running at him with outstretched arms. "Ezekiel!"

He wanted to introduce his future wife but after the initial sobs of joy and exclamations, he said the only thing he could say, "Why are you carrying a gun?" He was not opposed to constitutional liberties, he had just never seen his mother carry anything more than her 38 revolver. It was surprising to see her at such ease with an SKS.

She was still wiping away happy tears. "Sarah and I are on our way to help your daddy."

The Protector gasped, "You mean Daddy's alive?"

Zombies On A Plane

The frontline defenders could see a red, single engine plane with water skis flying at them from behind the enemy vehicles. Most were confident they heard a distinct pop from that direction.

They all watched, dumbfounded. The mayor knew exactly what was happening. "That's Mo!"

Kumar's distinct accent was heard radioing from his perch near the southwestern channel, "Plane dropped a..." he stuttered, trying to think of the right descriptor, "...bomb into rear of 40mm Cougar."

His report was drowned out by uproarious cheers and fist pumps by the defenders. The mayor could see machine-gun fire puncture the plane at several points from below.

The cheering tapered before the Phantom sounded over the radio. "Plane took several hits from LATV mount, landing on the east side of the island. Pilot does not appear to be incapacitated."

Randy grimaced, that was a good sign; he didn't expect Smokes to die. It was just difficult to stay strong in your faith when your sons could have just been riddled with bullets. Could Mo really just have rescued the island before being cut down at the doorstep?

He wished he had immediate access to a HAM-capable radio so he could message his son before the end. Randy would wait until this horrible day was over to tell Debbie what he had just seen.

There was absolutely no fire coming inbound to the island, all of the ground troops were racing to the armored vehicles and shooting at the rushing cannibals. At least five soldiers crammed into the Humvee and had driven to park behind the recently bombed Cougar. A few had made it to the MRAP with the disabled mount. A couple of pitiful souls were unlucky enough to seal themselves inside the grenade launching APC. The control for the 40mm had been obliterated, they were basically hiding inside a coffin that featured a disturbed interior design. Every single gun on the mainland was now aiming east and destroying any of the rabid nudists that came into sight.

He told his mother everything he could think of to tell her about his and Aka's journey from the prison to the front lines. Thankfully, the African beauty had been there to fill in anything he missed. The Protector was glad to see that his mother truly liked his fiancée. She was very interested when Aka began telling her about the hydroelectric dam near where she grew up.

Zombies On A Plane

Aka concluded her story by saying that she was pretty confident she would be able to get the electricity running here. Mrs. Collins stood on her tip toes in an attempt to put her arm over the much taller woman's shoulder. "I think we'll have to tell Randy about that!"

It just dawned on the youngest Collins male who this pretty girl traveling with his mother was. She asked, "So is Mo okay?" This was Sarah Ogle! He remembered her voice from the radio several days ago. Hadn't his brother been madly in love with this chick for years, but was too much of a pussy to ask her out? She at least cared about him enough to ask where he was. Maybe he could help Mo make some kind of move at the next opportunity.

The Protector answered with the sudden recognition making his eyebrows arch up. "Yeah, him and the other two went with that dude in the spacesuit on his *Apocalypse Now* boat."

His mother chided him. "That's Gene in Brotherhood of Steel armor on the Moldy Crow!"

The bodybuilder merely sighed as she "tsk-tsked" him. There was no way she knew any more than he did what either of those things were, she must've talked to Gene earlier. Easy was confident no one in his family could possibly be that nerdy.

"So if we send some assistance you will not fire on us?"

The reply came from one of the MRAPs. "Hell no, we're too busy with the damn zombies! If you give us a hand, we'll surrender and come out with our hands on our heads!"

Mo was incredulous. "I thought you were smart, Gene. This is the fucking stupidest idea you ever had!"

The tech lowered his radio as the boat began picking up speed. "Dangerous, not stupid. This is the most logical action and may result in the greatest number of lives being saved: both parties lending a little trust."

"Logic went out the window when people started turning blue and biting each other." Mo spit into the water before nodding to The Oracle. "And why we gotta trust these sumbitches with our lives? I'm sure there are some insignificant lives we could use!"

Smokes smacked a meaty hand on the engineer's armor plated shoulder. "Da Whiz gots some gonads!"

Zombies On A Plane

Mo could only slap his forehead in response. The Oracle had accepted this dumbass plan and was ready to rush headlong into the waiting sights of several machine guns. He was thinking that it was so much easier to have faith when your own life wasn't on the line. He was tempted to risk bacterial meningitis by abandoning ship and swimming to the island. Hammer began throwing lead at the peevies attacking The Villain. They had now gained a new ally versus the main antagonist whether The Hero trusted that ally or not.

The mayor turned and was about to greet his wife. He wanted to scream, to fall over, to start running at them. Walking beside her in his direction was his youngest son. This was one of the happiest moments of his life, directly following one of the worst. He walked to his son and realized he had only thought of Mo being on that plane. He firmly shook the younger man's hand and clapped him on the arm. "Easy."

"Mo's alive?"

"That's the same thing I asked about you! We thought you got shot or something when your radio went out."

Mayor Collins did his best to explain the unexplainable miracle that had taken place. His long-lost son continued, "He made it and he's with the Kathy Bates lady and the fat Chris Tucker guy–"

Easy was interrupted by his mother with the correction, "Captain Sledge and Marlon–"

He dropped his eyes to sheepishly smile and nod in acceptance even though he was pretty sure he had never heard that black guy referred to by that name. He guiltily picked up, "Are with Gene on the Moldy Crow."

At that moment a conversation between Gene and the military on the other side of the water started over the radio. Randy understood what was happening and offered to come across the bridge to do some "zombie cleanup" after the enemy surrendered.

Sally was on the verge of hysteria. "Jonathan!?"

Bobbitt could understand why his troops would offer peace, but knew he would ultimately not be accepted by these insurgents as a commander. If they continued fighting their human enemy, the peevies would eventually surround them, but if they allied with the humans they would be more likely to survive.

Zombies On A Plane

It was almost funny. Your enemy's enemy could only be your friend on one side because on the other side your enemy's enemy were insane cannibals. He couldn't blame his remaining men for choosing life, but was aware he himself would need to make a run for it. He could hear the soldiers bargaining over the radio and he was also willing to accept some help from the insurgents–until the time was right.

He continued blasting the blue monsters as he spoke slowly and between bursts from his mount. "Sally, we can make it out of this but you are going to have to do exactly as I SAY."

Javan Bonds

44

Mo Journal Entry 18

I WAS BEYOND astounded that every crew member of the Moldy Crow had not been diced into unrecognizable strips of flesh upon coming into range of the enemy's automatic weapons. We added to the continuous onslaught of bullets going into the ranks of the undead. It was strangely exhilarating to no longer be at war with the guys that had been shooting machine guns at us just moments ago, almost as if we had become their reinforcements.

Hammer lowered the cartoonish red and smoking barrel of the mounted 50 and stated the obvious. "Overheating. You boys care to give me some coolant?"

I've seen this movie. I probably could have worked one up at the time, I just was not willing to whip it out in front of Hammer. Yeah, I know she's a lesbian; she might even be more of a man than I'll ever be, and she wouldn't judge me.

I simply didn't think it was worth commanding her to turn around and start singing. "Nope, sorry, Cap." *We Were Soldiers* was the first movie that came to mind. Now, my excuse for not wanting to expose myself in front of The Expert would probably be that last scene from *Boogie Nights*. You know what I'm talking about and this is my journal, I can put whatever image into your head I want.

She turned to The Oracle who smiled sheepishly. He answered automatically, "I's dry as a bone; added a couple inches to da lake awhul ago."

She shrugged. I guess she saw the prophet take a leak into the water from the float of the Beaver earlier. The expert didn't bother asking Gene, that armor would be too much damn trouble to work himself out of. Her gaze returned to me. "Come on Mo, you can squeeze a little bit out."

What the fuck? I was about to tell her to do it! I was trying to give Mel Gibson an excuse when a lightbulb turned on. "Ain't this a fucking lake? Water's gotta be cold."

She nodded in agreement. She looked into the mounted ammo box and clicked her tongue. "There's only a couple rounds left anyway, not really a big deal."

Zombies On A Plane

What? I was about to accuse her of just wanting to see my pecker! She called back to The Tech, "Time to make landfall! Steer us to that pier."

Shit, I wanted to argue the usefulness of the two remaining shells; I felt a lot safer on a boat. Before I could speak, the three suicidal amigos were stepping onto the wooden planks and sending pain downrange.

I cannot count the number of times these people have nearly gotten me murdered. I guess I should credit The Screenwriter for the "nearly" part. If we were comparing the *Cora* crew to biblical disciples, I suppose I could relate to Doubting Thomas. I have no problem being a faithful follower when I am not at risk of being eaten. I'm sure I would deny Smokes three times if it would keep me safe. Well shit, I just realized that I'm not only a pussy, I'm downright blasphemous.

My compatriots were occasionally shooting peevies out of our sight. I took my own sweet time getting off the boat and creeping onto land. Sure, I've killed my share of zombies and I'm not really troubled by shooting the damned animals, I'm just not one of those people that go out of my way to kill countless enemies.

I played *Medal of Honor* back in the day–and yes, PC gaming is superior to your console, loser. Though I may have been too shitty an aim to be a sniper, I was a proud camper. Why would I run out into the open when you jackasses with the shotguns and bazookas would shoot in my general direction and kill me? I could just crouch in the corner with my BAR and wait! I'm nothing if not patient; I will let the rushing noobs clear a building before I go to find my perfect corner.

Four of the rabid nudists emerged from across the road to my east. They began screaming and howling as they charged me, blue private parts swaying in the breeze. It honestly would have been comical, naked people of all ages running and howling like lunatics, but the fact that they wanted to rend my flesh from my bones kinda sucked the funny from the situation. I'm not a Boy Scout and definitely would not have gotten a marksmanship award, but I dropped two of them with four shots and took aim on the third. Damn, the action clicked. Are you shitting me? I've never had a gun jam after so few shells. I dropped the rifle to pull my pistol with only yards to spare. I glanced to the right; I couldn't see my comrades and was too far to be seen by the men in the vehicles. One of the two remaining monsters lunged and I quickly pistol whipped the thing in the face before shooting the other.

Zombies On A Plane

The pistol whipped cannibal stayed upright and continued coming while its friend fell. I put two rounds in the chest of the creature as it closed its infected mouth onto my forearm.

"Oh. SHIT."

Javan Bonds

45

The Surrender

BY THE TIME the main group of defenders had breached the gap in the causeway and were crossing over onto land, The Expert and The Tech were zip tying each soldier's wrists as they came down the line. It was amazing that all of the soldiers had given up freely, throwing weapons out of the vehicles and surrendering with fingers interlaced over their heads. They seemed almost happy to be giving up, preferring living and being captured to dead or undead and free. The Oracle was keeping an eye on the perimeter with his shotgun at the ready as the mayor ordered some of the island dwellers to the mounted weapons. Rapid fire bursts tapered off to only the rare break in silence as the horde had clearly been decimated.

Sarah broke away from the Collins family and approached the ever watchful seer. "Where's Mo?" After coming to her belated realization that she loved him romantically, all she had wanted to do was see him and talk to him. She felt like she was just winging it, having no idea how it would go. She almost laughed, *that's what Mo always does,* she thought happily.

Smokes gestured to the east. "On da boat, lil' craka." The Love Interest began walking past him, feeling a pang of urgency to see her best friend. She heard a whisper, but never turn back to see The Oracle speak. "Mufuka ain't got da shit, yo."

Rather than ask what the strange soothsayer was talking about, she simply walked on without looking back. Mo didn't smoke pot; what "shit" could he mean?

Gene was confused when he came to the only person in the line of kneeling soldiers not wearing a uniform. "Sally Dick?"

She dropped her hands and began wailing. "Thank God! They've been holding me as a hostage! I've been praying you would come save me!"

Zombies On A Plane

The armored Paladin placed his hand on her shoulder as she wept uncontrollably. Bobbitt realized Sally was a decent actress and could have fooled even him. Though they had not worked out the details, he was hoping this would buy him time. She might not be able to escape with him, but her blubbering could be all he needed to make his exit to the LATV.

Hammer walked around The Tech to the next soldier in line, in no rush, but wanting to get a move on. She froze when she recognized the downturned face and thought about drawing. It was The Villain. The Expert gasped, "You!"

The Villain looked up and grinned, pushing her back as he stood, pulling his pistol. He fired, almost laughing. Knowing the body armor couldn't save her this time, not at this range. Sally followed his lead, pushing Gene back and sending a bullet from her 38 into his CHEST.

Javan Bonds

46

Mo Journal Entry 19

I HAD MADE it back to the boat, ready to push myself away from shore as soon as my color started fading. I was propped against the back of the boat with a pistol in my hand, unsure as to why I had not already blown my brains out. I knew I was not going to be human much longer; I wasn't betting I was immune or anything; I guess it's just instinct to be alive as long as possible. Maybe it was all part of the plan, like I was destined to become a fucking naked ape that hungered for human flesh. I couldn't bring myself to look at the bite, I had seen enough of them on others and knew it probably wasn't even similar to a bite out of a hamburger. It could be nothing more than a small break in the skin and I wanted to imagine I would die from a mortal and grotesquely huge wound, not a damn scrape. The initial sight of blood had been enough to make me realize that there was no point in checking or cleaning the wound

Why waste my few precious hours with personal hygiene when I can sit here and sulk about missed opportunities? It was a bit shocking that I felt absolutely no pain, there was blood and shit hanging from my arm but it did not hurt. I felt pressure when I was first attacked, but that had immediately faded to nothing, I wanted to go out with some class, in gut wrenching pain. Maybe the virus kicked in some kind of endorphins or adrenaline or something. I had expected unbelievable torture until I lost my mind and started ripping my clothes off.

I thought I heard Sarah coming from a distance. "Mo-Mo?"

I shouldn't have been confused to hear that voice as I died, probably in a sobbing heap. I questioned, "Sarah?"

She sounded happy to have found me and her footsteps moved in my direction. "Mo-Mo!"

She jumped onto the boat and spread her arms to hug me. She stopped and gasped when I briefly raised my arm to show her the injury. She nearly wailed, "Oh God! No!" She knew just as well as I did what made that mark.

Zombies On A Plane

She broke into tears as she sat down beside me and I put my uninjured arm around her shoulder. She began, "Maybe we...we can...take you to see the doctor..."

If I'm positively dying, I don't want to bother wasting my time. I firmly cut her off, "Don't."

The Love Interest exhaled shakily and just sat with me in comfortable silence. I spoke, "You know I love you right?"

"Oh Mo, I love you too."

I wasn't speaking of our platonic love, I was speaking of what I was sure absolutely no one else knew. I would be dead soon and had nothing to lose. "No, not like that. I mean I've been crazy about you since the day we met."

I reckoned then that she had already been aware of my devotion even though it was supposed to be secret squirrel. I had never admitted it to her, or to anyone. "I know," she paused before angling to face me. "And I have been, too."

Wait. This can't be what I think it is. Did she mean that she had been crazy about herself since the day she had met herself? It took me a second to realize she was saying that she felt the same way about me. A brief surge of pubescent rage flooded me. If all it took was my horrible death to get that answer out of her, I could've found plenty of ways to get murdered in the past decade.

Before I could speak, she leaned in and planted a brief kiss on my lips. That sent me into a greater panic than the fact that I would soon be a naked cannibal. "Sarah, what the fuck?" An exchange of body fluids with an infected individual means both parties immediately become infected.

That kiss was the only thing I had wanted for the past ten years. What should've been the greatest moment of my life was the exact opposite. I had just sent the woman of my dreams to the same blue grave I was going. Well, I didn't maliciously kill her, she used me to infect herself, I guess I can only be charged with involuntary manslaughter. Is this really how You answer prayers, God? You finally give me what I've been wanting just before I die but only if it kills the object of my affection?

She moved her face back and I nearly sobbed as I raise my arm between us. "We just exchanged body fluids!"

Zombies On A Plane

She shook her head with tears in her eyes. "I don't care. I don't think I could be here without…" She paused with a raised eyebrow and reached down for my forearm, gasping as she held it up to me. "Mo, it didn't bite you!"

I pulled my sleeve back to the elbow, it hadn't even ripped the shirt. I had popped the animal in the mouth before it came at me, I guess that's why there were teeth and blood on my sleeve.

We both began laughing hysterically. Neither of us was going to die and my completely evident secret was now out in the open. I drew her in close and wrapped my arms around her as she planted another, longer kiss on my mouth. I don't know if I was just being hopeful, but I'm pretty sure there was a little bit of tongue. Were we about to start fucking? There was no music, like I always hear in my dreams, nor was this was the safest location for that, being in the open with the risk of being attacked by other naked people, but I was game if she was.

I sighed as Sarah obviously realized the same thing. She stood holding her hand out to me. "Come on, let's go see your daddy."

I pulled myself up with her hand. "I'm hoping we'll live long enough to…wait, Daddy's ALIVE?"

Javan Bonds

47

Returning Hero

THAT WAS THE first time Sally had ever shot a gun. She liked how good it felt to kill one of these terrorists. The secondary betrayer smiled as he collapsed in a heap at her feet. Jonathan began running past her and she knew she'd better keep up with him.

Hammer staggered but remained upright, a little surprised she didn't have a hole through her. The Expert was angry that stupid commie used a metrically calibered round to splinter her collarbone. She raised her Pearl Handled 1911 at the retreating villain. "Hey Bobbitt." He looked over his shoulder, confused to hear the woman he had just terminated speaking. "I'm still alive!" She sent two bullets into his back and put one more in his collapsed form just in case.

Sally had remained frozen in front of the downed Gene. "What the fuck did you do that for? He was retreating, you fucking Nazi cunt!"

The Expert was about to explain to her that he was headed to a vehicle that featured a mounted machine gun. She simply settled with a scolding, "Language, missy!"

"Language? Fuck you fucking cunt! I'm a fucking Christian, goddamnit!"

The Captain was about to say something along the lines of "Sure seems like it," but suddenly, the former social worker leveled her pistol at Hammer. She quickly turned her still-smoking 45 on this traitorous girl and dropped her with one shot to the chest.

Hammer then sank to her knees as the defenders rushed to her side. She needed a break.

As they walked back to town, Sarah explained what had been happening over the past few days as far as she knew, clarifying that his father had only lost his radio, and was alive five minutes ago. The Hero and The Love Interest drew pistols and picked up the pace when two distinct shots came from the direction they were traveling. The action was finished and Hammer was on her knees as they approached. Mo heard Gene angrily pushing help aside from his prone position on the ground a few yards away from her.

Zombies On A Plane

"No, I will only have a bruise. But it hurt like a kriffing turbolaser!"

Mo had always assumed it was a cheap costume. "But how did it not get through the armor?"

"I told you I'm a sucker for replicas. I don't frak around with that cheap plastic poodoo." He tapped his now bullet scarred chest plate. "High quality steel reinforced with Kevlar. This would stop a blaster at point blank range."

Mo walked by The Expert, currently being treated with an IBD (Israeli Battle Dressing) and morphine shots from the nearest Phantom. "You're like a robot, Cap…err, Admiral," he smiled. "Bullets barely slow you down."

She cocked a thumb in the direction of the stiffening Bobbitt. "Yeah well, they sure slowed that Ruskie down."

"And it was that Bobbitt dude again?" He gestured to the deceased woman. "What about her?"

The recovering Expert blew her cheeks out. "That is—was Sally Dick. She lived on the island until a few days ago. The girl went missing and we didn't know what happened to her. She apparently ran into these guys up at the Armory and she was of the mind to get her way. Some of the soldiers say she was always jumping Bobbitt's bones."

He guffawed, "Dick? Bobbitt?" Mo paused and was met with silence. "Oh come on, nobody else made that connection? What if his name had been Harry?" After a few seconds, he made one more attempt. "Nothing?" He gave up after another round of crickets.

Leaving his teammates in care of defenders, Mo walked back to The Oracle and glared with respect. He asked accusingly, "You did it, didn't you?"

"Da fuck you talkin' 'bout homeslice?"

Mo croaked out, "You know. You saved my daddy."

Smokes only gave a benevolent and knowing shrug as Mo continued through the crowd gathering near the dock. The Oracle gleamed and knowingly nodded to his back.

Zombies On A Plane

The Hero finally found his father, who stopped his conversation with the commanding officer of the military unit. The Mayor smiled as he turned to his oldest. Slapping him on the arm and shaking his hand he offered, "Mo."

"Daddy. I told you we would bring him back."

Mo stepped back over to Sarah, still not sure what to do around her. He awkwardly put his arm over her shoulder and looked to the north. "Can we go home?"

She laughed and began walking with him in the direction of the *Viva Ancora.*

The Protector and his fiancée began following the two. After a day that took weeks, the sun was finally setting to their left. The couples came off the causeway and onto the island proper at an easy pace. A greeting came from the direction of Best Western. "Howdy pilgrims."

The Hero almost asked, "Is that you, John Wayne?" but saw no cowboy hat. Dr. George walked in their direction in a singed and dirty doctor's coat.

"Well shit doc, you missed out on all the fun."

The Phantom cardiologist smiled. "Not really. I was avoiding a grenade launcher and then maintaining sniper over-watch. I saw you take the Cougar with a grenade. Good job by the way."

Mo was willing to take credit for something he didn't actually do. "Thanks, I try."

"I know it was Capt. Sledge that dropped the grenade."

"DAMN."

48

Mo Journal Entry 20

DR. GEORGE PARTED with our little band soon after joining and headed down to the clinic. I don't know what the hell is wrong with us, especially me who has been doing this shit for at least a month, but we all thought it would be a good idea to fucking walk across the island. We don't have to worry about nudists eating us, but modern transportation seems to remain the farthest thing from our minds. The four of us actually walked past dozens of bicycles, and not one of us suggested procuring a mode of transportation besides our own fucking feet. Almost all of the inhabitants had gone to defend the island; it was nearly as quiet as my first quest to retrieve condiments. Only the noise of birds gave realism to the scene.

I turned to Sarah. I had to ask, "So why did the birds come back?"

"No idea. It's less creepy when you can hear them though." This country boy had to agree with her.

We continued down Gunter and passed the courthouse, to my beloved ship. The girl to my side offered, "I guess I'm going to need to move my stuff onto the *Cora*."

All I could do was smile like an idiot. She actually just said she wanted to move in with me. Holy shit! I almost fist pumped as I thought about what would happen next. I've only had one girlfriend move in with me and her XXXL clothes barely fit into the damn chest of drawers!

Wait, girlfriend? Can I actually call her that now? I've been sharing the same residence with an unrelated female for over a year now and I sure as hell wouldn't think of her as anything more than a crewmate. I guess it depends where she sleeps. Sarah, not Crow! Shit, now my boner is confused.

When we came to the next block, The Old Friend was rolling out of his gym and noticed us.

"Easy!"

They raced to each other with massive arms spread wide, the rekindling of a long-lost bromance. They faced each other and it somehow wasn't awkward for a tall, insanely muscular bodybuilder to give a sitting down, insanely muscular bodybuilder a dude hug.

"Why weren't you out shooting soldiers?"

I rolled my eyes, he was probably teaching some young girl how to work her glutes. "I figured your daddy had everything under control and I was doing some cardio anyway." Figures. "But I was just about to head that way and see what I could do."

"They pretty much got everything wrapped up. Don't worry about it."

Bradley nodded and gestured to the woman at my brother's side. "And who's this lovely creature?"

"This is Aka, my smoking hot fiancée." He grabbed her ass, continuing to fill Bradley in on everything.

I began pulling Sarah along. "I reckon we'll get on while y'all catch up."

Like he just realized there were other people standing only feet from him, Bradley greeted me with surprise. "Mo, glad to see you made it back, man!"

We nodded our farewells as the paraplegic with a monkey on his shoulder ushered my brother inside. "Dude, I've got to show you my set up in the weight room, it's pretty sweet!" I could just picture that scene from *Dude, Where's My Car?*

The rest of the walk was uneventful with me not knowing what to say and Sarah comfortable in our silence. I think I was actually afraid to speak to the woman that had just declared her love for me, despite the fact that we had known each other most of our lives. I didn't want to say anything to piss her off. I don't even remember what I said to Eternity to get her to move in with me. I guess I didn't have to say much to convince a fat and horrible person to get free room and board for a year. She was pissed all the time regardless of what I said, so I couldn't really use my last relationship with a white and barely female version of Smokes as a precedent. I think I'll just wing it; that never turns out awkward or embarrassing!

Zombies On A Plane

"You still working at that diner?" I questioned like an idiot seeing a friend or former schoolmate on the sidewalk.

"Yeah. I make pretty good tips there."

That was the meat of our conversation. She didn't seem to have a problem not talking; she had always seemed to be just as comfortable as me in silence. I think that's one reason I have always been insanely in love with her. I think I will enjoy being in this relationship, less of a chance for me to say something retarded and fuck things up. I guess that means it's time to start discussing politics!

We had nearly reached the *"Cora"* without my realizing it. I dropped my head and face palmed before I looked up and screamed for the cook. "Crow!"

After several attempts, the American Indian woman looked down at us. "The fuck you want, white boy?"

"Yeah, it's nice to see you too. Let us in!"

She dropped the rope ladder over the side and I pinched the bridge of my nose. I whispered to The Love Interest, "Can we just move to the courthouse?"

"Well…"

I interrupted The Love Interest with a wave of my hand, just realizing that I had suggested we move back in with my parents. "Nevermind."

I turned my face back to the cook above us. "You do know your girlfriend got shot again, right?"

"You fucking with me, white boy?"

I tried not to smile as I shook my head and Sarah agreed with me. "Yep. She took a round in the chest."

Crow moved like I've never seen her. She expertly dropped the gangplank and ran right past us. "Mother fucking white people, I kill all of you!"

Well, I'm willing to get Hammer shot every day if it means I don't have to risk falling to my death on concrete. "Petunia's white, by the way!" I couldn't resist shouting back at her as she ran to be with the woman she loved.

Sarah–my new girlfriend–and I made our way from the deck and to the captain's quarters where I sat on the edge of my bed. I awkwardly stammered, "So what now?"

Zombies On A Plane

There was a gleam in her eye and she slowly sauntered in my direction. "Oh, I don't know."

"Well, we can always go down to the courthouse and get some of your–" she shoved me down onto my back. "I've been waiting for this for a long time, Hero." I think I can figure out what comes NEXT.

Javan Bonds

49

Mo Journal Entry 21

FOLLOWING OUR SEVERAL hours of passionate lovemaking–read that as Tim Meadows with a lisp and an Afro–okay, it may have actually only been a few minutes, but remember, this is my journal and I record things the way I want to. Anyway, Sarah and I were lying on the bed when my radio sounded. "Mo, this is Gray Fox. You read?"

I reached over my girlfriend's naked form–yes, I'm going to remind you of that every chance I get–to give a reply. "Loud and clear, Daddy. What's up?"

Though his transmit button was off, his sigh was nearly audible. "Can you come to the main deck of the *Cora*? You need to be in on the post-op briefing. Over."

"Yeah, I'll be up shortly."

I untangled myself from the woman of my dreams, who was naked, by the way, and began quickly dressing. You know, I'm surprised my dad didn't just walk into my room and start telling me what was going on. Maybe Smokes or my father's spidey sense let him know that I was occupied. It's funny, guys do seem to have a sixth sense that tells them when another guy should not be bothered. Well, except when I walked in on Easy the other day. If you remember, nothing embarrassing ever happens when someone just walks in on me, well, except for the two instances I mentioned earlier. Damn. I would have been proud in this instance, though obviously it saved my completely nude girlfriend some awkwardness.

"No, I wouldn't really call them prisoners; they're not villains or anything. They were willing to be bound and remain overnight on a yacht. Once we are sure they weren't infected, they will need to be integrated into our society. We can't treat them differently."

I shot back, "It won't be that easy. They killed quite a few people!"

Zombies On A Plane

My dad was adamant for forgiveness. "I know, I was there. They were taking orders from a lunatic with a grudge and have all renounced their former United States postings. If these soldiers swear allegiance to Guntersville, it's a huge win for us!"

My dad and The Oracle sat across from me at the roundtable. They discussed with one another as I read the written report.

This report told of Hammer's stable condition after a gunshot to the chest that would have killed a normal human. She was now being sewed up at the clinic by Dr. George, the report went on. The Phantom doctor had been assumed lost by the other defenders, being unable to make radio contact until returning to his office. I snickered, vividly picturing Crow screaming at the doctor, "Fix what these motherfucking white people have done!" There were several more technical entries on weapons and vehicles salvaged after the battle with Cock-No-More. I scanned through it to discover that we captured twelve soldiers, three personnel carriers, one Humvee, and a LATV. I don't know who would be willing to clean up the grenade launching MRAP, but at least it was no longer in enemy hands. It really would be a good thing to have that many trained defenders, once they had proven they could be trusted.

According to the casualty report, the island had lost seventeen defenders–all of the main protagonists and the full Phantom squad had survived. Damn, I need to give Smokes or The Screenwriter some credit for keeping my ass alive for another journal. Daddy told me about Georgia, that she had recently moved in with The Tech but had perished. That sucks. As a man I am legally obligated to secretly wish that Gene got laid before she had been killed. After some investigating, they found that the murderer was a new immigrant, Earl Buckalew. Haven't I heard that name before? I would have to ask about that one later.

I set the papers down and pushed away from the table. My dad added to report on the others I cared about, "Your mama's getting ready for bed at the courthouse, your brother and his fiancée are gonna stay the night with Bradley. Bro. Williamson stayed at his ranch throughout the fight. Gene did a hell of a job; he's back home at Excelsior. Oh, and we are planning to take Aka to the dam tomorrow; she may be able to power the entire island. You got anything planned?"

I had a living woman that actively participated in doing naughty things. "Actually, I don't think I can make it."

Zombies On A Plane

My dad shrugged and turned to The Oracle. "You got anything to add, big guy?"

Smokes stood with a straight back and I was expecting some kind of cryptic prophecy detailing how we would have to endure some new terrible shit tomorrow. My tension dissipated as he spoke casually, "Hell naw, cuz. I'm a get me some sleep!"

We broke from the meeting, exhaustion evident in all of us. I questioned The Oracle.

"How long until the next Reason?"

The professor answered as he approached the stairs.

"When it's time, you'll know."

Damn, now I'm almost too creeped out for sex.

ALMOST.

Javan Bonds

50

Chief Engineer Gene Stanley's Log 4

THE DAY OF the great battle for independence turned out pretty stellar for the island as a whole, but for me personally, it was the worst day ever. I lost my soulmate, my Padme', my Imzadi, my Trinity, and I will never be able to replace her. Hunter is grieving rather well, having lost two parents in such a short time. He is a tough little youngling. I believe I am still in a state of shock, not yet throwing Klingon curses at random passersby or drinking myself stupid on Corellian brandy. I'm in a state of strange calm. I wonder if the Elusive Man from *Mass Effect* survived the zombie apocalypse? We could try Lazarus to resurrect Georgia.

It's funny how things seem to happen almost as if they are scripted. The original crew of the *Cora* made it through this ordeal, Mo completed his quest and returned with his brother, and the doctor is currently studying a living peevie. He may not produce a cure, but I'm hoping he can at least discover what has made them adjust to walking in the fraking sun! What has miraculously turned them into day walkers? Solutions of vinegar produce attracting qualities; perhaps we will discover zombie repellent in alcohol or some other solution. I'm sure more answers will come the longer he studies the creature.

The sniper team that nearly put a hole through the mayor was clearly attacked before they lost all communication. The soldiers reported hearing screams and cries of "Mayday" before they dropped off and remained forever silent. We have our cardiologist / NSG Phantom to thank for that.

No mortal can explain everything; why did Randy fall at the instant he did? His radio being destroyed midair proves the bullet missed him by millimeters.

Ezekiel Collins's future bride claims to have knowledge about the workings of hydroelectric dams. She is slated to travel to the TVA dam with nearly a company of armed soldiers to attempt to re-electrify the island.

Zombies On A Plane

I have not been without electricity here at Excelsior, but I am excited for others to have power. I'm pretty sure I can start at least a local broadband system. I am going to be schooling noobs in no time!

As we sail off into a recently re-ordered, peaceful galaxy, I must ask: Can the Center hold, or is this just the calm before the STORM?

Javan Bonds

Epilogue

Thud

It was finally free from what looked like the head of an animal. Had no scent, did not move, even after it had worked its teeth through whatever was over its mouth and tried taking bites from the thing. It clearly could not be an animal. It was finally on the ground now and its memory of getting into its previous position was fuzzy. It could not remember anything about its past, not even its name. It had simply become conscious a few hours ago, wrists trapped together around a large fake animal. Its first priority was to get these bonds from around its hands so that it could strip and defecate freely, as nature intended. The female had no idea why anything would want to cover itself and constrict the flow of feces.

As it kicked the covers off its feet, it noticed an apparent bite mark on the back of its ankle, swollen and festering. It couldn't remember any recent fights. It shook its head; suddenly feelings flooded its mind; a distant memory of "before." It was consumed with a fierce, illogical rage.

Its new goal suddenly became clear: feast on live flesh. The image of its targeted prey appeared and it had a name:

"COLLINS!"

Zombies On A Plane

Javan Bonds

Zombies On A Plane

The Following Is An Excerpt From Book 4 Of The Still Alive Series

ROBERTO MARTINEZ WALKED along the road and remained in direct sunlight. He stayed away from the Diablos in the shadows, but was always ready to dive into the ditch if a hostile enemy or a vehicle approached. He was one of those that escaped Jefe's place when it was first attacked. After spending a few days in Albertville searching for surviving familia and coming up empty-handed, he was now returning to Douglas and discovering mostly scorched earth. The houses he had passed in Albertville were not completely destroyed, but they certainly were here.

He knew what was under the charred remains of Jefe's casa.

Bob remembered seeing the medico making his way back to Jefe's bedroom when the federales started shooting. He wasn't sure who all knew about this underground bunker, but would be glad to find the doctoro still hiding down there. He moved a few pieces of crumbling word and found the manhole cover which opened to a ladder.

This passageway would lead down to the safe room. Bob pulled his trustee pistol from his belt as he opened the door to the shipping container. The mechanic was greeted by nothing but pitch black. He lifted the mini flashlight on his key ring and saw the place was empty. All the safes were opened and gutted. There were none of the lights he had seen when Jefe had originally shown him this bùnker for hideaway. Surely, those pindayhose had found this place and raided it.

The diminutive mechanic turned to make his way to the door with disappointment hanging over his head. His light ran across a package of MREs and a case of bottled water. As he continued to the door, his flashlight settled on a note taped to it. "*Viva Ancora* with Mo – Randy Collins."

Bob spent days turning the note over in his head: "Viva Ancora?" The he was fairly certain Jefe didn't speak Spanish and wouldn't know that "Viva" translated to "alive" and he had no clue what the other word was, it wasn't Spanish and he was pretty sure it was in English. Maybe Jefe was simply trying to send some kind of encrypted message that he was still alive and Bob could take piece in that. He set up from his makeshift bedroll when the realization struck him: "Viva Ancora," wasn't that the name of the boat Jefe's skinny kid worked on?

Zombies On A Plane

Bob could've sworn to Madre Maria the that the kids name was Mo! Maybe the kid would give him a tour once he got there. After another few days of living in this luxurious cave, Bob would attempt to make his way to Guntersville Lake and hopefully discovered the Jefe Familia on a boat, safe from the monstrous.

The round little Mexican might not look incredibly healthy, but he knew how to be conservative with his food and survive. Supplementing the freeze-dried, packaged meals with squirrels, nuts, berries, and fruit, he could stay here for as long as he wanted.

As he picked up a few pecans from beneath the largest tree near the road, he heard distant explosions coming from the direction of Guntersville. Not knowing exactly what and only that something was happening down the mountain, he decided to wait a few more days before making his journey to the lake.

He decided to wait a couple of dias to begin his long walk down to Guntersville. He hoped to find Jefe safe from the blue monsters. Before exiting his home of the past few weeks, Bob stuffed the remaining bottles of water and MREs into his pack.

The handyman fixed the note in his gaze. His handwriting was worse than Jefe's chicken scratch. He could not recall the last time he had been forced to write in English. Even so, the short repair man made his sloppy mark below the first inscription. "Still alive going to Guntersville beginning of June Bob."

If he was to die on his way, maybe this note would be found by the former owners of this casa. They would eventually find this note where he had found it originally and understand what happened to him. He made it up the ladder and started the trek.

Bob felt like a bandito each time he had to force his way into a house . He had to break into a home every night when the sun started going down. He knew he wasn't committing a crime, he was not breaking in to steal . Even though he did take the occasional can of sardines or bottle of Coke. The reason had to do with getting shelter from the loco animale outside.

The whiz with small engines passed the Shell station and continued down the mountain. He was almost there. About halfway down the incline, he began hearing explosions from in front of him. Bob squinted and could make out military vehicles sitting on the mainland side of the causeway, facing the island.

Zombies On A Plane

Were the federales attacking more innocent people? He wasn't sure on which side of the land bridge lay the protagonists and which side held the antagonists. The diminutive mechanic decided to make his way over to the apartment building on his left. As he made his way across the highway, a small plane zoomed overhead and passed over the vehicles. One of the trucks opened its rear door and an explosion of meat, blood, bone, and everything else one would expect to see from an exploding sardine can of humans violently shot out the back. The smaller truck over to the side sent some shells in the direction of the plane and it began smoking. The obvious water plane started its final dissent on the east side of the island. Bob could only wonder who just been shot down.

The short repair man jimmied the lock on one of the doors to an upper story apartment just as screaming, naked people started charging the military trucks. He thanked Dios for keeping him out of the hands of the criaturas outside. At least he could watch the scene at the bottom of the mountain from a rear window.

It was shocking to see the Diablos in the daytime. Even more surprising was witnessing the things attack armored vehicles.

As if their hunger drove them to the point of insanity, one would run full on one of the vehicles to be ripped into shreds by a mounted machine gun. Another would follow right behind to be slaughtered in the same fashion. Chunks of mutilated infected were strewn all around the vehicles.

A few soldiers would occasionally walk up, completely ignored by the creatures. The soldiers would blow the back of infected, unsuspecting skulls to the ground. Bob had been informed by television that the Diablos would pay no attention to a newly infected human, he was sure the soldiers must've already been bitten.

Vehicles started coming from the island side of the causeway and mowing down more of the animales. He wasn't sure what was going on. The federales began to exit their armored trucks and get down on their knees in obvious surrender. After at least a dozen soldiers in line had been searched and cuffed, the searchers came to one smaller person and simultaneously an infantryman. They were obviously surprised to have found these two. The soldier in question rose to gun down the redheaded woman in front of him as the other person shot the armored man. Both of the shot fell and the soldier began to run away.

Zombies On A Plane

The redheaded woman rose up on an elbow and gunned down the retreating soldier before beginning a short conversation with the smaller individual which she then shot. The armored knight stood up and people began rushing to the injured woman as she again collapsed.

This was interesting. Bob would observed for a few more days to try and get a feeling for these defenders. The diminutive mechanic wasn't willing to rush headlong into villano. Bob would gladly wait and see.

It appeared the federales had not overtaken this Alamo. The battle scene had been cleaned up within a day or so, the human cleanup crews only gathering up human bodies or equipment. Strangely, the morning after the battle, every single blue corpse had mysteriously disappeared. The repairman began cautiously making his way down the mountain in the middle of the road. Almost to the causeway, he took in several stop- and caution roadsigns driven into the pavement or hanging from telephone wires.

"Hands up! Approach slowly." a synthesized voice sounded from somewhere in front of him.

Bob dropped his pack, slowly raised his hands in surrender, and walked forward. He was still not sure if these people were with Jefe or if they were banditos.

Either way, he was fairly certain that they were not federales, so he supposed it could be worse.

They could have simply chewed him up with machine gun bullets with no warning. Bob was perplexed to see a man in a full suit of armor and a sword over his back standing behind a small shack on the other side of where the bridge used to be. The guard asked over a loudspeaker if he was armed, if he was alone, where he had come from, his name, and several more questions he would expect to be asked from an immigration officer. He guessed he had given satisfactory answers because the Jet Ski pulled a pontoon bridge over and he walked across. The mechanic noticed a gaping hole in the side of the hotel.

He had so many questions about what was going on here and who these people align themselves with. The only thing he could think to ask was a simple question. "RANDY COLLINS?"

TO BE COUNTINUED

LOOK FOR BOOK FOUR IN THE

STILL ALIVE SERIES

COMING SOON!

Zombies On A Plane

Follow Mo and His Fellow Survivors in the

STILL ALIVE SERIES

PICK UP

BOOK ONE:

ZOMBIE LAKE,

BOOK TWO:

ZOMBIE ISLAND

AND COMING SOON

STILL ALIVE:

BOOK FOUR

Available on Amazon, Coming to B&N, and Other Book Outlets in Multiple Formats Soon!!!

Javan Bonds

Follow Javan Bonds and keep up to date on

upcoming books and events at

www.javanbonds.com

Like Us On FaceBook

Or Contact Us At

zombie@javanbonds.com

Zombies On A Plane

About The Author

Javan Bonds is the author of the newly released apocalyptic zombie series *STILL ALIVE,* and the bestselling *Free State of Dodge.* Bonds has had to overcome numerous obstacles in writing as well as just living his daily life. Diagnosed at the age of 11 with Friedreich's Ataxia (FA), (a progressively degenerative neuromuscular disease under the umbrella of the Muscular Dystrophy Association), he has slowly been robbed of his physical abilities through the years. Bonds became wheelchair bound in 1999, but that was only the beginning of his setbacks. His sight began to diminish in 2010 and he is now legally blind. His hearing began failing to the point he now can't distinguish individual voices in a noisy room. In spite of all of this, he continues to consume three to five audio books a week as well as work on his future novels.

Bonds never lets his disability rule him; he has lived fully, loved, and laughed often. Reading and writing has long provided Bonds with both pleasure and a creative outlet. He began blogging at a very young age and has published articles and letters for his local newspaper. In 2010, he discovered a passion for writing novels and with help of Nuance's Dragon Naturally Speaking, he writes every day.

Javan Bonds

In late 2015, at only 28 years old, Bonds was told he may have only a short time left due to the ravages of FA on his heart. Since learning this, his goal has been to complete a significant, lasting body of written work before his time in this world runs out.

In mid 2016, Bonds published his first full length novel: *FREE STATE OF DODGE*, the first in a dystopian series about an America in decline and its rebirth.

He is currently publishing the fourth book in his zompoc humor series, *Still Alive*. The series is currently set for eight books. Javan and publishing team, hope you enjoy his work and all of the upcoming books in the *Still Alive* series.

Javan has these words of wisdom to offer others stricken by a life shortening illness:

"Live your life. Light your candle on both ends and let it burn. It may burn out faster but your flame will burn brighter than some who live much longer"

Keep an eye on his flame, watch it burn!

Zombies On A Plane

Javan Bonds

Made in the USA
Lexington, KY
28 January 2018